SCHRÖDINGER'S DOG

Martin Dumont

Translated from the French by John Cullen

OTHER PRESS • NEW YORK

Originally published in French as *Le chien de Schrödinger*
in 2018 by Éditions Delcourt, Paris.
Copyright © Éditions Delcourt, 2018
English translation copyright © Other Press, 2020

Production editor: Yvonne E. Cárdenas
Text designer: Jennifer Daddio / Bookmark Design & Media Inc.
This book was set in Goudy Old Style by
Alpha Design & Composition of Pittsfield, NH

1 3 5 7 9 10 8 6 4 2

Library of Congress Cataloging-in-Publication Data

Names: Dumont, Martin, 1988- author. | Cullen, John, 1942- translator.
Title: Schrödinger's dog / Martin Dumont ; translated from the French
by John Cullen.
Other titles: Chien de Schrödinger. English
Description: New York : Other Press, [2020] | "Originally published in French
as Le chien de Schrödinger in 2018 by Éditions Delcourt, Paris"—Title page verso.
Identifiers: LCCN 2019025749 (print) | LCCN 2019025750 (ebook) |
ISBN 9781635429985 (paperback ; alk. paper) | ISBN 9781892746290 (ebook)
Classification: LCC PQ2704.U58 C4813 2020 (print) |
LCC PQ2704.U58 (ebook) | DDC 843/.92—dc23
LC record available at https://lccn.loc.gov/2019025749
LC ebook record available at https://lccn.loc.gov/2019025750

TO MY MOTHER

"Some renowned philosophers—

such as Schopenhauer—have declared

that our world is exceedingly ill-made and unhappy,

and others—such as Leibniz—

have found it to be

the best of all possible worlds."

—ERWIN SCHRÖDINGER

PART ONE

1

There's someone on the other side of the wall.

I don't think I was asleep. Dozing a little, maybe. I'm lying on my back, I haven't opened my eyes.

The floorboards creak, someone's slowly approaching the bedroom. I'm not sure. Maybe I'm still dreaming.

The footsteps move away toward the kitchen. Seconds drag by, and now I no longer hear the slightest sound.

Suppose it wasn't Pierre?

It's possible, after all; it could have been a burglar. A skillful, well-trained sort of fellow—I didn't notice anything that sounded like an entry. He may have picked the lock and then gently opened the door.

It's easy to verify. I can just get up and go to see. I could even satisfy my curiosity by calling out; Pierre will answer if he hears me. The thief, on the other hand, will flee the scene. In either case, I resolve the doubt.

If I want to know, all I have to do is act.

So why am I staying put?

It's strange, this impression I have: the feeling that I would spoil everything. Because there's an equilibrium to consider. At bottom, it's almost a game: someone's walking around on the other side of the wall; it's not Pierre, it's not a burglar; it's as if they were superimposed. Yes, that's it. As long as I don't make sure, it's a little bit of both.

2

In the end, I sat up. My reflections seemed stupid. Maybe the idea of a burglar had ended up worrying me—I don't know. Let's just say that I wanted to see my son.

I got out of bed and checked the clock. I'd hardly slept. I sighed, thinking I'd pay for that at the end of the night.

As I was leaving the bedroom, I saw Pierre. He was sitting outside on the balcony. He'd put some cookies and a glass of milk on the little iron table.

Pierre is twenty and never misses an opportunity to snack. When I point this out to him, he shrugs and smiles.

I poured myself a cup of coffee in the kitchen—I can't stand milk. I've always liked cookies, but the things he eats are too sweet for me. By the time I joined him, he'd already finished half the packet.

"Hey, Dad."

He smiled at me with a cookie in his mouth and then asked me how my day had gone.

In the course of the morning, I'd picked up several fares at the airport, all of them bound for the center of town. Most of my customers had never detached themselves from their phones; the others had slept with their heads against the window. I'm no longer surprised to hear them start snoring as soon as they've settled into the back seat. In the early afternoon, I came home and went to bed.

None of that was very interesting, so I simply answered "Fine" and asked him the same question.

Pierre's a third-year biology student. He gave me a detailed description of his day. After lunch, he'd gone to his drama club. Not that he likes the theater, exactly, because Pierre doesn't ever attend plays; he prefers to be one of the performers. He's been that way since he was little.

He'd spent the afternoon with the club. I don't understand why he never seems to have classes. Sometimes I ask him for an explanation, but he gets his back up and says I've never been to a university. "You can't understand."

His troupe is preparing a new production. "An original work," he specifies. He's the author.

Pierre really likes to write. That's been the case for longer than I can remember. When he was younger, he used to fill up entire notebooks.

He talks to me about his play and I nod, because he's told me the plot about ten times already. His eyes shine while he recites the scenes. Rebellion, friendship, fear, and justice. Also love. His concoction contains a little of everything.

"You see, Dad? You should read it!"

I have no excuse. He printed out the text for me last month. I promised to read it, and it's been lying on my night table ever since.

He describes the rehearsals. He gestures dramatically, accompanying himself with exaggerated movements. He laughs a little, but his face hardens when he talks about the leading actors—a couple, if I've understood him right.

"The guy—he's just out of his depth."

The girl, however: a monster talent. He can already imagine her on the screen. I suppose she must be pretty; long hair, angelic smile, good student. My Pierrot always falls in love with the girls at the top of his class.

I figure he'll go on about her for a while, but I'm wrong: in a flash, he returns to his critique of the leading man. This time, it's more scathing. His diction's bad, his acting grotesque. And he's got a big head to boot.

"He thinks he's a star!"

I can't help smiling. Pierre blushes. He says, "Yeah, right, I admit it. I'm jealous." And he starts laughing.

After that, he clears the table. His cheeks seem a little gaunt. It's as though he's gotten tired all of a sudden, and slightly feverish. When I ask, he says no, everything's fine. "It's almost the weekend. It's normal to be a bit exhausted." I don't insist.

. . .

It's *Thursday*, so he's going out. I don't even ask where he's headed. It's the same thing every week—I've grown used to it.

I'll go on duty at ten tonight. In the meantime, James Bond is on TV. One of the films with Roger Moore. The human zucchini. Pierre laughs when I say that.

I heat up two slices of quiche, but he won't take one. He'll stop and get a sandwich on the way. He kisses me and puts on his jacket. "I'll be home late, maybe even after you." I'm not supposed to worry.

When the door bangs shut, I freeze for a few seconds. In the kitchen, the quiche is ogling me through the glass door of the oven. Ah well. I'll eat both slices.

3

I think I was really in love with Lucille. Put like that, it sounds weird. The first years were great. It's hard to understand how it could all have gone so wrong.

When I met her, she already had her humanitarian side. She was a member of several associations, she donated a lot of money. To fight hunger, war, AIDS. There was also that thing with the panda.

It irritated me to see their self-satisfied faces when they persuaded her to sign up. Automatic withdrawal, fifteen euros a month: the orphans thank you. I never liked the guys who did that sort of work. Cultivators of guilt: "Look me in the eyes when I talk about poverty and squalor." They targeted Lucille because she was weak. You didn't have to observe her for very long to figure that out. Watch her eyes for a minute, maybe less. A sadness heavy enough to split concrete would come back at you like a boomerang.

Me, I wanted to take her in my arms, but not those boys, not them: real vultures. Without an ounce of shame.

They circled around her, salivating. "You see that one, the one lagging behind a little? There could be a way to get something out of her."

Well, all right, maybe that's a caricature. I used to laugh at Lucille, but affectionately. I'd scold her for being naive, because, after all, I thought it was pretentious to want to change the world. But I always let her go ahead and try. She loved doing that, and it's a passion like any other.

I didn't see the moment when she went over the edge. With hindsight, I tell myself that I might have been able to do something. At least in the beginning, when she began to escape me. But I had to work too much, and the kid, even when he was two, still took up an incredible amount of space and time. Besides, the difference wasn't all that noticeable. I mean, she'd always been that way. Fragile, too sensitive. Not sad, no, but melancholy. Yes, there's a word I like a lot. Melancholy.

Her doctors didn't say it like that. "A disease," they said. It had a name I didn't want to remember. A problem inside the head, something ultimately invisible. It's frustrating, because it's so hard to imagine.

Of course, her penchant for misery hadn't escaped my notice. Woe always came upon her in phases, marked by long periods of sighing. Nevertheless, I fell in love with her, because you can't control everything. Maybe I liked being able to help her.

When she was sinking into depression, I played the clown. Sometimes she'd smile.

On the days when all went well, there was such joy—it's impossible to explain. I believe you have to go through pain before you can really enjoy the good times. Pierre's birth had made her so happy. It was such a beautiful success. Concrete proof that what we had could work.

In fact, I always thought we'd make it through. Maybe I still do. It wasn't a big problem. It made life a roller-coaster, but life's often like that. When you hit bottom, you brace yourself and push off to climb back up. I found out a whole lot of things by suffering. Misery has its place; if it batters you, you can leave it a little room.

When Lucille started spending time with her group, I didn't get it at first. I didn't see the difference. Her groups, her associations, those all seemed to me to be more or less the same old story. Pierre was little, and I thought she needed some freedom. I was confident we'd make yet another comeback.

I was wrong.

When she stopped eating fish, I wasn't surprised. She didn't like meat. Then came eggs, milk, honey. She would talk about nature with spellbound eyes. At the time, she used to say she'd been a dove in a former life. I don't think she believed that, but she put her heart into it. In any case, it remained a circus, and it made me laugh a lot. One day when she was biting into a tomato, I told her she might be chowing down on my father. The fruit caught me right in the face.

So that was how she got inside her circle. From that angle, I mean. But it wasn't just a vegetable affair. There was a guy. He said his name was Yalta. A lot of it revolved around him. I soon figured out why they didn't eat anything, considering what they were treating themselves to...though I never knew what it was. Something mind-blowing, without a doubt.

My Lucille, in the underworld. I can see her now: easy meat. She dove in head first, and by the time I realized it, it was too late. All the same, I got her out of the fix she was in, because you can't act like a total idiot. I remember Yalta when my fist landed on his nose. He cried like a child. After a stay in the clinic, Lucille came back home. I did all I could, but I'd already lost her.

4

I drove out of the parking lot early. I didn't turn on the radio right away. First I had to decide.

Always the same questions. Run out to the airport? With all the arriving flights, I'm sure to pick up some fares. Of course, I have to get in line and wait, which I always find unbearable. Going out there guarantees an unpleasant evening. But in the end, the pay is adequate, and that often makes all the difference.

I could also cruise for fares in the city center. It's double or nothing. On good nights, I do really well, but the demand is too unpredictable. Sometimes the city's deserted and I drive around for hours. I've always secretly wondered: is there someone who decides for everyone else? "Tonight, boys and girls, we're staying home." And why does the decider always forget to inform us?

The best idea, no doubt, would be to trawl around the bars. I can very easily be satisfied with that. A little later in the night, I'll even wait outside the doors of some of the clubs. It's risky—passengers have vomited on my nice leather seats—but it brings in a little cash. And besides, young people have some good qualities. They talk, they laugh. They're never too drunk to make conversation. And that's always more pleasant than the guy who spends the whole ride hanging on his phone.

I haven't always done this. Cab-driving, I mean. When I first got here, I hung around the markets. At the time, there was work to be had in the stalls. I made a living unloading merchandise. You had to get there very early to make sure you got hired. Sometimes, weather permitting, I'd sleep out there. I would bring along a sleeping bag and lie down in a covered area of the market. It wasn't so unpleasant; there were often other young guys with me.

That was how I met François. A super person, always friendly and kind. He'd bring along thermoses of coffee and share them with me. At night, we watched over each other so we wouldn't get robbed. We'd take turns sleeping. In the morning, the first one who spotted the stallholders would wake the other.

As time passes, people end up trusting you. Two or three times, I filled in for the vendors. It was hard, and I don't think I was any good. Finally, I put some money aside and got a driver's permit, because doing that would open doors for me. I became a deliveryman; it was nice, I liked being at the wheel, but in the end I quit that job too. I couldn't stand my boss. The kind of guy who yells nonstop and sticks you with impossible schedules. I've never been one to let people yell at me.

I learned that some taxi drivers were selling their licenses. François found out all about it, and we discussed the opportunity. He'd already borrowed enough money to start as soon as possible. I was tempted, and the plates weren't all that expensive. There wouldn't be anyone giving me orders. I let a week go by, and then I took the plunge.

I can still remember the day I got my license. I was so proud. When they handed it over to me, I immediately thought of Pierre. I couldn't wait to show it to him. He was little, he'd just turned four. During the day, I'd leave him with Madame Alves, an enormous Portuguese babysitter who took in as many as five children at a time. I would pass by to pick him up around six o'clock, at the end of my delivery shift. That evening, I was terribly late. I'd waited a long time to pick up the metal tag, and then I'd had to have it attached.

Night had already fallen when I rang the doorbell at Madame Alves's house. She opened the door, and the first thing I saw was the relief on her face. I didn't give her time to bawl me out. I seized her hand and covered it with kisses. "Forgive me, forgive me, Madame." I kept repeating that, and she didn't know how to react. Then I saw that Pierre was right behind her. I threw myself on him. His eyes were red—he must have cried a lot. I lifted him up and carried him out to the street. As I ran along the sidewalk, I could feel his little hands tightly clutching my neck. When we got to the car, I put him down and knelt beside him.

"Look, Pierrot. That's Daddy's car, that one."

He didn't answer, but I could see his eyes open wide. I think he understood. I could feel warmth rising in my chest.

I picked him up and put him on the hood. Now, from where he was standing, he had the roof light right under his nose. He smiled, and I swear I saw the four letters reflected in his shining pupils.

TAXI.

The beginning of a new life.

After that, we spent more time together. I could make my own schedule. During the day I often took him with me in the car. Seeing a kid in the front seat of a cab would amuse the customers. I don't know if I had the right to bring him along, but it doesn't matter. I never had the slightest problem. Later, he started going to school, and things became simpler financially.

As he grew older, I was able to leave him alone at night more and more. That was when I started my nocturnal work routine. I'd give our neighbor my keys, and she'd look in to make sure the kid was asleep. Working at night allowed me to see him during the day.

These days, when I get tired of sitting alone in my taxi, I try to remember those.

5

I ended up heading for the center of town. I figured I'd take my chances—waiting wears me out too much. I couldn't spend any more nights inside a stationary car. The kind of absurdity that can make you crazy. If you drive around, at least you get to see the city go by, and that's already something.

I worked three hours and knocked off. It was a bad evening; I didn't have the heart to persist. I hadn't accumulated more than one hour's worth of fares, not even enough to cover my expenses. To salve my conscience, I swore I'd spend the following week at the airport. I turned a corner and thought I saw a raised arm. Tiredness was stinging my eyes, so I couldn't be sure. I stepped on the gas to chase away all doubt.

Back at the apartment, Pierre was asleep on the sofa. The TV lit up his white face; there was a plate of pasta shells on the coffee table. I smiled as I took in the scene.

Pasta, that was one of his big theories: "The best way to avoid a hangover."

I cleared the little table and shook him. With an effort, he opened his eyes. "You're back already?"

"Yeah. I got sick of it."

He smiled. As a matter of fact, he likes it when I knock off early. For almost two years, he's been insisting that I should quit. "Night shifts are dangerous," "You work too much," that sort of thing. But I like working this way. Time is suspended at night; there's less noise, less traffic. And then there's the nighttime surcharge added to every fare, by no means a negligible amount.

I was surprised to find him sleeping there. When I asked him what time he came home, he shrugged. "I don't know, I was tired."

He added something about a stomachache.

"From alcohol, right?" I said, teasing him.

He smiled and swore he hadn't had a single drink, and then he went to his room.

It was twenty minutes after three. I didn't have the slightest chance of falling asleep. I got a beer out of the fridge and sat in front of the television.

The next day, I drove to the university to pick up Pierre when he got out of class. When I pulled up, he was having a discussion with some friends. I sounded my horn. He shook hands all around and walked over to the car. After putting his bag in the back, he got into the passenger's seat. "It's all good," he said. I stepped on the accelerator, and the car surged onto the street.

I drove fast. I've always liked that. I was in a hurry; we'd been talking about this weekend for some time. Three days together, just the two of us, with the sea all around. Time passes fast, and such moments are rare. I know it has to do with age. Children grow up and drift apart from their parents; it's in the order of things.

After some traffic slowdowns on the suburban roads, I turned onto the expressway. We started rolling along at a good clip. Pierre smiled at me, and I asked him how he was doing. He told me he was tired. "But delighted to be here!"

He talked about his day, and then he slid over to the topic of the novel he'd been trying to write for months. "I'm getting close to the end."

He talked to me about revisions, about some last details that needed changing. He was almost finished.

Then what, I asked him. He kept quiet for a while, his eyes fixed on the road. Then, with a wink, he said, "I'm going to send it to a publishing house and win a lot of prizes."

I laughed, and so did he. "You'll see, you'll see," he said.

I pointed out that he wanted to become a biologist, but he just shrugged and said, "One doesn't rule out the other."

I agreed, because what he said was no doubt true. I didn't remember ever hearing of any writer-biologist, but

I knew nothing about that sort of thing. I remembered that Pierre also used to talk about making a career in the theater. All the same, it's really something to be twenty years old...

We talked some more, and then rain started to wet the road. Some sunbeams were striving to break through, but the cloud cover slowly overtook the horizon. I switched on the windshield wipers.

"I thought the forecast said good weather."

Pierre turned toward me, laughing. "We're going to get wet in any case, right?"

6

I've always liked diving. I can't remember when it started. My father used to take me out in the early evening, after school. Our house faced the sea, so it was easy. The first times we went out, I was too young, I stayed on the surface with a mask on my face. I'd watch him turning below me, and the sight would give me incredible dizzy spells. I still have the same impression today. To dive is to fall, but it's a fascinating fall. An intoxicating loss of balance.

Pierre got hooked right away. At first, I was glad of that. My father, me, and then my son. Something was being passed down, a part of the family saga. Later he joined a specialized club. He'd made a lot of progress.

He often said his fondness for biology came from his diving. He talked about specializing in the study of the ocean floor. I understood; it's awfully beautiful down there. But hard to describe properly. You have to experience it, you have to slip down into the dark waters. Seriously, it blows your mind. Often enough, you don't feel like coming back up. You have to be wary of euphoria.

When I was a teenager, my pals and I went diving every day. We dove as deep as possible to impress the girls. We flirted with disaster. When I think back on it, we were assholes. But we didn't give a damn—underwater was where we felt best. There were always things to discover. The local oldsters called us "mullets" because we'd turn up in the port sometimes. They would holler at us to get out of there; the water was disgusting, they'd say. I don't know. None of us ever got sick, and there were lots of pretty sights down in the roadstead too. I've always thought boats are more beautiful when seen from underneath. Well, that was then, and there's no chance I'll go diving in the harbor anymore. When you see the shit floating around in there these days...Things were different back then. I think.

I missed all that a lot after I left. The sea, to start with—it was hard for me to be so far from it. And then the silence. I mean, when I went down, the bottom wasn't the only thing I was looking for. Immensity is also on the inside. I've always loved the moment when your heart slows down and calm spreads into your very muscles. That was how I would stifle the frenzy of the rest. Life, my anxieties—all that external noise. Out of the water, I've never really been at ease.

One day I explained this to François, and he talked to me about *l'ivresse des profondeurs*, "depth drunkenness," the rapture of the deep. I hated that word, "drunkenness." It wasn't that. Sure, I like to get smashed sometimes, but when you drink, your speed increases. Your body's working at a hundred kilometers an hour. Besides, that's what you're looking for, isn't it? Fire in your eyes, and in your guts too, if you want to come on to a woman. Underwater, it's the opposite. If you dive down there, it's for the calm. Maybe you'll go crazy, but it's never like drunkenness. It's ecstasy.

Good, but all the same, it takes training. I remember one day, I must have been fourteen. I was hanging around the port when a motor scooter came up and stopped in front of me.

"Are you Yanis? Is it true you can dive down ten meters?"

"I can go deeper than that."

"Ten meters'll be enough. Get on."

We went through three villages and ended up on the big pier. There was a group of guys who all looked to be around twenty years old. One of them came over to us. He was deathly pale.

"You can dive deep?"

"On a good day, down to twenty meters or so."

"And you could find a coin underwater?"

That stopped me cold for a few seconds.

"Yes or no?" the guy asked, getting worked up.

"Take it easy, Félix."

One of the other young men put a hand on his shoulder. The one called Félix moved away, grumbling. The other guy explained what was up: it wasn't really about a coin.

Félix had gotten married the week before.

"A hell of a party," his friend recalled with a smile.

The next day, Félix had a handsome wedding ring on his finger. The ring had belonged to his grandfather. "Kind of a symbolic thing, see?"

A few days later—the previous evening, actually—Félix and his pals had gone out. A way of proving that nothing had changed.

They'd taken a boat out to the Island, dropped anchor in a cove, and spent the night drinking until sunup.

"A classic evening."

The problem was that Félix had lost his wedding ring in the water, no one knew exactly how. Stupidly, just like that.

I didn't have time to ask for details. They seemed to decide that I was capable of finding the thing. I boarded the Zodiac with them and we charged out to the Island. Félix pushed the motor to its maximum speed, and the boat banged against the waves. The sea was gorgeous, not too rough, just a great swell with a rippling surface. I stared at the horizon and saw a white triangle standing out against all the blue.

The cove was sheltered from the wind. I thought that was a good thing, and I concentrated. It was hard to clear my head with all those guys yammering around me. The only one who kept quiet was Félix. He looked at me pleadingly, and I smiled at the thought that he might be scared of his wife.

They applauded me after I reached the bottom on my very first dive. The depth wasn't even ten meters, eight at the most. I told myself that as divers, these boys must really be pretty bad. On the sea floor, some little clumps of algae were growing among the grains of sand.

I swam along the bottom but didn't see anything. Gold on sand, not much hope. I went up for air three or four times, and I could tell the guys were getting more and more upset. So I started pushing myself to stay down longer. I pressed my head against the sea floor, and a sense of fullness slowly pervaded me. I became all-powerful, untouchable, in control of even the least of my muscles. That particular osmosis is something indescribable. The fuller I became, the more I felt a desire to go farther. I could leave them all behind, I thought, them and their wedding ring and their insignificant anger.

And that was when I saw it. A stroke of luck, because I'd stopped looking for it. It was shining in the light. I picked it up, and the emotion I felt ruined everything. Adrenaline wrecked my equilibrium; my heart started beating again and reclaimed its rightful portion of air. My tense muscles made a fin stroke, and my body rose up. All the same, I paused before breaking through the surface. Held one arm above the water, the ring tight in my fingers. Thought I'd impress them a little.

I don't clearly remember what went on next. The boys were so happy they wanted to celebrate. The ride back to the pier was even faster than the ride out. Félix sprang for about ten rounds of drinks, and by three in the afternoon, I was already vomiting.

Pierre has propped his head against the window and fallen asleep. Outside, the rain has stopped. I feel good. Many things come back to me in this moment. When he was little, I used to put him behind me, buckled up in the middle of the back seat. He'd stay awake the whole trip; getting him to go to sleep was impossible.

He put me through hell, that kid. The hyperactive type—no naps, no downtime. And look at him today, snoring for the past half hour.

In the end, it's never completely lost.

7

It took us four hours to reach the seacoast. No matter how much time has passed since I moved away, it's always been hard for me to live so far from the water. Pierre didn't grow up like me, city life is the only life he knows. He likes the sea, even adores it. But he doesn't miss it.

We often spend the first night with Lucille's parents. They live in a house on the coast. It's practical, and it allows Pierre to see his grandparents.

Personally, I've never had the least doubt. Those people hate my guts—it's a thing you can feel. So much resentment is hard to get past. I think they hold me responsible. For their daughter, and for unhappiness in general.

They have no qualms about displaying their hatred. Especially the old lady, quite a nasty piece of work. After Lucille went, I really thought they were going to snatch my son away from me. Fortunately, the law is well made. They couldn't take him. The judge announced his ruling with a weary look on his face, and I was pretty damn happy.

After that, we calmed things down. For Pierre's sake, mostly. Deep inside, I think he's very fond of his grandparents. He never objects to visiting them. Generally, we spend one night there and leave the next day, but when he was younger, I'd let him stay with them every now and then. It was hard, I could never hold out for very long. I'd go to pick him up, and it did me good to see their faces when he got into the car.

As soon as we arrive, the dog drags himself over to us. I say "drags," but even that's an overstatement. He's an old spaniel, fifteen years old, in fact, senile and half deaf. A clump of fur that's been on the verge of croaking for I don't know how long. He's suffering; you'd have to be blind not to see it. I'd use my rifle on him, but I'm afraid the old man would shoot me next.

The old lady served us chicken for dinner. She almost never talks. Papi's the one who makes conversation. Stopping him is not a possibility.

We were attacking the dessert when he started talking about his daughter. He can't restrain himself. He twists the knife in my wound, every time. I'm well aware that it's eating him up too, but there's nothing to be done. On the one day when I begged him to shut up, he'd called me a monster and accused me of staining her memory. I almost jumped on him, but I held myself back. For the kid, and for Lucille too.

I have to say that hearing such things bothers Pierre considerably less than it does me. He never really knew his mother. I'm not saying he didn't suffer, but that's different. He can listen, though, and I think he likes it. After the cake, I took my glass and went outside.

I walked down to the beach. To tell the truth, it was more like a cove, a chaos of sand with rocks scattered more or less everywhere. Foam whipped the ensemble without letup. I listened to the crashing waves. I could barely see them. A moonless night had fallen, the horizon was black as pitch. I inhaled the smell of the tide. I realized how much I missed everything about sea spray. I imagined I'd come back to all that water one day, and then I sighed. You tell yourself so many things. The cold caught up with me, and I crossed my arms against my chest.

When I went back, I saw that everyone had left the table. The old woman was just about finished clearing it. I thanked her and carried the bags upstairs. Pierre was in the bathroom, vomiting.

"Is everything all right?" I called to him.

The toilet flushed. I heard him unbolt the door, and then he appeared, his complexion pallid. I repeated my question. He nodded: "Yes, it's better now. I don't know what came over me. Like a sudden urge to puke up everything."

"You have to see a doctor."

He started joking around. "You don't think the probable cause was Mami's cooking?"

I insisted, and in the end he promised. The color was already coming back into his face, so I felt relieved. He wished me a good night, and I watched him disappear into his room.

We got up at seven o'clock the next morning. Pierre grumbled a little when I woke him. I went downstairs to drink some coffee while waiting for him to get ready. The old folks were up; he was reading the morning paper. I sat down and poured myself a cup. Papi didn't lift his eyes from the page. I didn't exist; okay by me.

Pierre joined us to eat his bread and jam, dunking the slices in a bowl of hot chocolate. The old man put down his newspaper and stared at us. He asked why we didn't do any spearfishing. "I can't believe you don't when you can hold your breath for so long." He added that if he could dive, he wouldn't have any problem spearing one or two sea bass.

Pierre smiled because it's the same old tune, every time. It's beyond his understanding—the grandfather's, I mean—that you can dive for the sheer pleasure of diving. I even tried fishing once, but the spear gun just got in my way. And besides, I don't like fish. I'd just as soon leave them in the water.

Pierre's attitude is different. He's "against," opposed to the whole idea. He says you dive to enjoy the show, not to spoil everything. He gets excited and puts me in mind of Lucille. Which is always a strange sensation.

He stood up to his grandfather. It even seemed to me he called him an "old jackass," but I'm not sure. In any case, the old man chose to let it go.

We left the house an hour later and drove to the port. There we got on a ferry bound for the Island. Loading the car had reminded me of the first time. Lucille was twenty-five years old and pregnant. We were going through a good patch; pregnancy suited her fine. I remember her face as she watched the old cars vanishing into the belly of the boat. Of course, she had taken a ferry before. But the old one, the one that used to carry her to the Island when she was little, was much smaller. It could take only two cars, which parked on the deck in the midst of the passengers.

That was why the new ferry made such an impression on her. It was much larger and much faster. There was a parking garage inside it, capable of transporting up to fifteen vehicles per trip. The garage door, which opened on the side of the boat, was a big metal plate. When lowered down onto the landing stage, the door served as a loading ramp.

"We're not going to sink?"

She'd asked me that question in an intimidated voice. I laughed gently, not making fun of her, and promised her we wouldn't.

Once we were on the Island, we headed for its southern coast. That's where we always go diving. The cliffs are unrestrained, they just plunge into the water. The view above the surface is lovely by itself, but you have to look below too. The land falls away everywhere, dozens and dozens of meters down, and then the slope smashes into the sea floor. There are rocks covered with multicolored coral and crevices throwing enormous, soft-edged shadows. To dive there is to blend into the nuances of the world. All you have to do is hold your breath a little.

They've built a hotel on the cliff. A modest little place, it offers no more than a few rooms. You'd think it was a private home. They don't accept reservations, but they always have a vacancy, even in high season. That's the way it is, I can't figure it out either. Maybe people are afraid. When you look out over the sea, you notice a lot of things rising to the surface.

We said we were going to go out for a dive before lunch and left our bags at the hotel desk. It wasn't the best time of day for diving, but we wanted to warm up. We'd go back again, later in the afternoon. When the daylight starts to wane, the fish come out to hunt.

Pierre led the way to the beach. I walked behind him, and it amused me to observe his gait, the way he stepped. With the passage of the years, he'd acquired a slight forward lean, as if refusing to grow too tall. Sometimes I point this out to him, and he grumbles and says, right, he knows, he doesn't hold himself straight, so what?

Down on the beach, we put on our suits and entered the water to get good and wet. Then you have to go back and lie on the sand for a little while. Ten minutes or so, just for stretching. It's the neck that's most important. And we always perform breathing exercises to slow our hearts.

Pierre did all that with great diligence and closed eyes. We went back to the water and finished equipping ourselves. Flippers, masks, snorkel tubes. You always slip a knife into its sheath on your leg, and you always wear a lead belt; additional kilos are essential to good diving.

Pierre went in first. He gave three kicks and then veered toward the rocks. I spat into my mask—to keep it from fogging up—and followed him.

The first dive of the day is never very pleasant. You have to get used to it; your body takes a little while to acclimate. The pressure increases, the cubic meters of water weigh on you more and more. And then your heart's beating too fast; you suck in some of your backup air supply, and the signals aren't long in arriving. The deficiency, the physical distress you can't bear much longer.

Nevertheless, I needed only three fin strokes to reach the bottom. My system was getting up to speed. I slipped along a rock and spotted Pierre ten meters to my left.

We stayed in the water for less than an hour. I didn't want us to push ourselves too much, we had the whole day. We went back and lay on the sand, which was now much hotter, and then we took off our gear to let it dry on the rocks. I'd left a bag with sandwiches and bottled water in the shade. We sat down and devoured the mayonnaise-soaked bread without exchanging a word. It was often like that: at the end of long apnea sessions, you need a little time to come back to normal.

After lunch, I lay down for a sunbath. Pierre was sitting cross-legged, bent over a little white book. I watched him for a moment. It was an amusing sight: he moved his lips as he read. Would I hear him murmuring if I crept closer to him?

Finally, he raised his eyes. "Will it bother you if I work on my book a little this evening?"

I shook my head, and he smiled. "I can't wait to finish it. I've got the whole thing in my head. It's an obsession!"

I tried to remember when that had started. There had been so many things he was passionate about. That was the sort of kid he was, always getting carried away with everything. Well, all the same, it seemed to me he'd taken up writing while he was still very young. Maybe when he first got to middle school. True, he'd always written little texts here and there. One day he gave me a short story for my birthday; he must have been thirteen. It was about a diver who tries to recover a fabulous treasure. The chest is hidden in a sunken ship, so the guy has to dive really deep. In the end, he reaches the treasure by hanging on to a dolphin. I'd been happy to discover, back then, that the subject of diving interested him.

"You talk about free diving in your book?" I asked.

He smiled. "Not this time, Dad. Sorry."

I shrugged and then closed my eyes for a brief nap. I felt the sun warming my skin. A little below us, the sea rolled lazily over the sand.

The light started to fade around five in the afternoon. I'd had time for a siesta. Pierre was asleep a little farther off, just in the shadow of the cliff. I shook him.

"Shall we go back in?"

He looked a little foggy, but he got up. We put on our equipment again and started straight down from right in the middle of the rocks.

It didn't take me long to feel completely at ease. I was quickly able to descend to about fifteen meters. I knew it would all come back to me. I kept an eye on Pierre, and he on me; one of us was always above the other. Blackouts never really give you any warning.

I was following a big grouper when I felt Pierre's hand pulling on my leg. He signaled me to go back up, and I followed him.

"What's the matter?" I asked after we surfaced.

"Can we stop?"

"Already?"

He made a face. "Yes. I don't know what's wrong with me. My back hurts, and I'm tired out. I can't dive down and stay down."

I was surprised, but I made no comment. I raised a thumb, and we swam back to shore. We changed clothes in silence and left the beach.

I let him take his shower first and stretched out on the mattress. Actually, I was frustrated because I hadn't had time to forget myself. After all, that moment of letting go, that's what you're looking for down there. The pressure's finally off. The discomfort, the lack of oxygen: everything dissolves in the water. Then and only then, there's nothing left, and you let yourself go.

Pierre worried me. It was rare for his dives to be shorter than mine. Ordinarily, he descended without difficulty; he could go down as far as twenty meters, he could hold his breath for more than three minutes. Today, I hadn't seen him stay on the bottom even once. I blamed him for going out so much; he must have picked up a virus or caught a cold. I had eagerly looked forward to this weekend with him, and it annoyed me that he was sick.

The hotel restaurant seemed more like a living room. A fireplace, a couple of wooden tables. In low season, the owner always waited on the tables herself. I had the impression that she recognized us, but I wasn't sure.

We ordered the plat du jour. Pierre got up to go to the men's room, and I looked over my surroundings. There weren't many diners. It was a calm place, and I liked being back there. Agitation exhausts me. I think that comes from spending so much of my life in a taxi; you stay alone long enough, you get used to peace.

Our dinners were served, but Pierre still hadn't come back from the toilets. I felt something in the pit of my stomach. Light, but disagreeable. I took the napkin off my lap, and that was when I saw him. He was moving toward me, looking stunned, his face transparently pale. No, more like strangely yellow.

He came closer. His whole body was shaking.

"Dad..."

I didn't recognize his voice. There were too many groans, too much fear inside it. I felt my heart racing in my chest.

"What? What? What's going on?!"

The owner came up to us. I'd knocked my chair over when I stood up. Or maybe it was the table, I don't remember anymore. I grabbed him by the shoulders.

"Pierre! What's the matter?" I shouted.

He kept staring at me wide-eyed.

"In the men's room..." He was mumbling, I had trouble understanding him.

"What happened in the men's room?"

I felt him tense up.

"It came out white."

8

When the doctor arrived, I was surprised. I'd been prepared for a long wait, but we were in the room for only a few minutes, sitting rigid, side by side. He politely asked if I was coming, and I stammered. In fact, he was addressing Pierre. He'd spoken to him directly, without even looking at me. His manner was professional, maybe a bit ceremonious. Pierre said yes and got up, and I followed suit.

We sat on iron chairs, facing a big desk. The doctor took a seat on the other side and put his notes in order. He seemed to hesitate; he was practically squinting, his eyes darting from Pierre to me as if he couldn't decide. I started feeling uneasy. Maybe he was just getting warmed up.

Finally, he lowered his eyes to his pages again. He read the figures in silence, nodding.

I gazed at Pierre. There was nothing to read on his face, not the slightest expression. He was waiting, and I decided to imitate him. Through the window, a little courtyard was visible. A well of light, with four walls a few meters apart. Brilliant rays were falling into it. I wondered what the sky looked like.

The doctor coughed, giving the signal: he was ready. Pierre started to make a movement but then changed his mind. He looked so nervous that I asked myself how long I'd been staring outside.

"The results aren't good."

That came too fast. I wasn't expecting it, not even after the coughing. I mean, I didn't think the announcement would come so directly. Pierre fidgeted. I saw his lips move, but I didn't hear anything. I put my hand on his and signaled to the doctor to go on.

There was something. A spot, a growth on the head of the pancreas. Further tests would be necessary; the doctor suspected complications. The white stools—they were the reason. There was also dark urine sometimes, but that wasn't systematic. Pierre's fatigue, his vomiting, his backaches: they all had the same explanation.

"It's a tumor. It's too soon to say how far along it is, but we must react quickly."

The silence that followed was, I believe, deliberate. He was giving us time to absorb the information.

Pierre's hand began to tremble against mine.

Tumor.

I compensated for the trembling by squeezing harder.

The doctor started to talk again, and his timing was perfect.

 39

"Whatever the level of seriousness may be, an operation is necessary. From the looks of it, it seems possible to remove the whole thing. That's a good point."

I gave Pierre a smile, a tense smile. He wasn't looking at me.

The doctor talked about the operation: "Major surgery, but the techniques are well understood." He spelled out the risks: 80 percent success rate. He asked us what we thought. I say "us," but he was gazing at my son. There was no more hesitation, neither in his voice nor in his eyes. Pierre, on the other hand, turned to me. I could see the fear spread across his face.

"I . . . I agree . . . If it's necessary . . . Right, Dad?"

I averted my eyes. I was ashamed. I couldn't bear to meet his. I said yes, of course, we agree. The sooner the better. The doctor nodded, looking grave, and then he smiled. "I'm going to perform the operation myself. Everything will be fine."

There were some more complicated details. Date, anesthetic, allergies. Pierre answered the questions, and I tried to concentrate. That made my forehead hot, and I had trouble breathing. I looked into the courtyard, but a cloud was obstructing the sun. Not a bright spot to be seen.

"Dad?"

Pierre shook my arm, and the doctor repeated himself: "Is it all right with you if your son comes back to the hospital tomorrow morning?"

Tomorrow. The word resounded inside my skull. I murmured in agreement. After that, I sighed a long, slow sigh. I felt panic coming on, and I didn't want it to show.

"Perfect, we'll meet again tomorrow."

He stood up and gave us his hand. A smile was fixed to his lips. It was comforting to see how self-assured he was. He accompanied us to the door of his office. I stepped ahead and didn't see Pierre's face. The sounds of our footsteps echoed on the staircase. We were suddenly alone, and I had to speak. I was terrified. I settled for going down the stairs and turning around from time to time.

The air outside was like a slap on the nose. We took a few steps, and I put my arm around his shoulders.

"It'll be all right, my Pierrot. I..."

I didn't finish my sentence. Pierre had raised his eyes— they were filled with tears.

I pulled him close, and he slumped against my shoulder.

Back home, I regained my calm. I tried to reassure him and then cooked us something to eat, talking about the progress of medicine as I did so. I don't think he was listening to me. He wanted to know. What did it all mean? Because, after all, the doctor hadn't said a whole lot. A tumor, yes, that sure sounded bad, but he hadn't said "cancer." Was there a difference?

There we were, too alone and too ignorant not to torment ourselves. We were going to have to get used to it. Nobody would say anything—at least, not right away. There would be other tests and careful, rigorous diagnoses. But all the same: they were going to lay him on a table and open his belly. The doctor had been confident, which counted for a lot. But how about afterward? Would that be the end of it?

Surely not. So why hadn't he clarified anything?

When Pierre became insistent, I told him to calm down. I didn't know any more than he did, and it was eating away at me just as much.

I clowned around for him, and it made me think about Lucille. It was strange. I often did that for her. Maybe that's all I've got. An outdated weapon, a glass wall.

It was pathetic, but I kept it up all the same. Pierre smiled once or twice, so I scored a few points. When the meal was over, he went out to see some friends. To my surprise, that made me feel good.

I got after the dishes, humming a familiar tune. My hands shook in the stream of water from the faucet. I felt the walls closing in, and so I sang louder. Blood rushed to my skull, my heart raced in my chest. I thought that I'd suffered with Lucille, and how, but I'd never been afraid. It took Pierre to scare me to death. Whenever he came home too late, whenever he was gone too long. After a while, I learned to recognize it. That anxiety, that terrible frustration: as if all things were determined to slip away from me.

My son. Only he could put me in such a state. My brain raving, my imagination shooting off in a thousand directions at once. You find yourself making up all kinds of nonsense. He always wound up coming home in the end, and I'd get annoyed at myself for having worried so much.

A dish slipped out of my hand and broke in the sink. I watched the water running over the broken pieces of crockery.

Maybe this time was different.

9

Pierre entered the hospital at eleven in the morning. Operation tomorrow. I stayed with him the whole day. They served him a light midday meal. He wasn't hungry. We talked, the two of us, mostly me. Nobody came in to tell us anything; I had no idea how much time he would spend here. I offered to bring him some books to read, but he declined. "I'll be too tired." I insisted, and in the end he gave me a list of novels.

The surgeon came to see Pierre in the afternoon. He explained the operation to us. He went through the whole thing, every step. He spoke well, but there was too much distance. I mean, the words he used, they were no doubt the right words. And the details too, they were helpful in reassuring us. He knew what he was doing. And yet, I'd been expecting something more personal. Why didn't he touch my son? He could have sat down beside him, could have made a gesture; that would have been warmer. But he remained standing at the foot of the bed, and his voice resounded too far away from us.

A few moments later, he left the room. I felt like following him into the corridor. There were so many questions. I restrained myself so as not to upset Pierre. I stayed at his side, and—finally—he fell asleep. Seeing him so tired made me feel guilty. I hadn't seen anything coming. The weeks when he'd been so exhausted, the backaches he'd complained about, the vomiting. He was my son, I spent my time looking at him. But I had missed the only thing that really counted.

It was almost seven in the evening. I stood up and walked over to the window. The sun's last rays were lighting up the walls of the hospital. A shimmering orange veil settled over the buildings. I've always loved the fading light of day. The final parade, a lap of honor, and then the night.

The nurse came in to tell me that visiting hours were over. I could come back tomorrow; the operation was scheduled for the early morning. I thanked her and leaned down over Pierre. He'd woken up and was silently observing me. I wanted to hug him, but I restrained myself. I never do that sort of thing—I'm afraid it might be too solemn.

I ran my hand through his hair. There was a gleam in the depths of his eyes. Not fear, no. Maybe a little apprehension. I thought he was pretty damn brave. I told him so, and he blushed slightly.

"Good night."

Out in the corridor, everything seemed smaller than it had when we got there. I took a little tour to see if I might be able to find the doctor. All I saw were a couple of nurse's aides, two women who were clearing away the meal trays; they smiled at me as I passed. I went downstairs with an old man. In the elevator, I realized that he hadn't even noticed me. Everything seemed so familiar to him; he must have been coming here for a long time.

It was cold outside. The night had won in the end. I walked to my car. Not far away, the main thoroughfare was roaring with traffic as people left work. Since I didn't want to go home, I turned on my roof light. I felt better at once—my taxi often has that effect on me.

As I was pulling out of the parking area, a woman raised her hand, and I stopped.

She didn't wait long before starting to prattle away. Ordinarily, I like passengers who talk. But in this case, I was sorry I'd picked her up. I wanted to concentrate on myself, on my hopes and fears. I needed to let my brain analyze the situation, fabricate the future, reflect on what could happen to us. Rising to the occasion would require some imagination on my part.

Of course, there was no way that the woman in the back seat could know any of this. She just kept on telling her story. Her husband was the reason why she was there. "It's hard to recover from a heart attack at his age."

I understood completely, but I didn't give a damn. I muttered, "Yes, yes," as experience had taught me to do. Her voice was too loud. I couldn't think.

"He will recover."

As to that, I should have no doubt. A sturdy fellow, her Léon. And besides, his time wasn't up yet. "The problem is physical degeneration. He's always been a force of nature." My own father too, that's the type of guy he was. A bear. My mother liked to call him that. But Léon didn't like anything about losing his strength. "It's terrible, you know? He needs a nurse to help him relieve himself. That's what's wearing him down, having to depend on other people..."

When we reached her destination, she left me a big tip. I thanked her and wished her good luck. She walked away. I watched her go, because there was an incredible dignity in her step.

10

I hardly slept at all. Because of the operation. Also because I often work at night. I got up at three a.m. to switch on the television. There wasn't anything on, but I stuck it out for an hour. When I went back to bed, I picked up Pierre's play, which was lying on the night table.

I don't read, or when I do, it's newspapers. I had trouble following. It was the story of a kid going off in search of his mother, who died during the war. He makes his way to a village and conducts an investigation. I smiled when I read that the boy's father was a taxi driver. I wondered if that had been Pierre's idea. It was possible, and the idea gave me pleasure.

I imagined him, alone in his white room. Tomorrow, a stranger would cut his stomach open. I don't know whether I was nervous about that. Maybe just awestruck. A hospital is a hell of a thing, all by itself. It radiates uncommon power. I'm a guy who's always had confidence in medicine.

With Lucille, it was a different story. Conspiracy theories, that sort of thing; she trusted neither doctors nor medications. When she talked about the pharmaceutical industry and its lobby, she'd work herself up into a terrible state. The interests advocated by Big Pharma were the diametrical opposite of hers. She was crazy about acupuncture—she taught me the word while sticking a cactus needle into my skin. "It's good for you," she said.

I never had any doubt about my Lucille's good intentions. If she could have relieved all the suffering in the world, she would have.

I just wish she would have started with herself, at least a little.

At the hospital, they told me Pierre wasn't awake yet. He hadn't even returned to his room, so I had to wait. A nurse's aide promised that the surgeon would come by and see me.

There was a smell I couldn't identify in the waiting room. A remarkable smell, but without the least character; there it was, it could be perceived, and yet it wasn't anything. Clean and impersonal.

I don't often go into hospitals. Not more than the average, I mean. Once or twice with Lucille, when her crises were at their peak; but she hated the hospital scene too much. In the end, I stopped trying to persuade her.

The more I think about it, the more I realize I gave in a lot. I couldn't say no. That's why it was my fault too.

The doctor wasn't showing up. I understood, of course; emergencies take precedence. In my case, I didn't have any valid reasons—or yes, maybe I did, but not reasons like that. There were surely some fractures he had to deal with, likewise some hemorrhages. As for me, all I had was distress, anxieties racing back and forth through my brain. I couldn't hold that against them; the ache I felt inside was already too far gone.

The hours were passing, and I was going crazy. Just before I got up to yell at the receptionist, the doctor arrived. I said nothing, of course. A hand was extended, and I gripped it. The surgeon smiled the way you'd smile at nobody in particular. It didn't mean anything. I had to make an effort, because my heart was beating too hard.

"Will you follow me, please?"

I thought he was going to his office, but instead he accompanied me to the room. When he stepped in, he looked all around, as though surprised to find it empty.

After a few seconds, he invited me to sit in the armchair while he leaned against the wall. I was very uneasy. His body loomed over mine. This position—him above me—made him look like some kind of professor. He began to explain the situation. Pierre was doing well; he'd wake up in an hour. Then they'd bring him back to the room.

The operation had gone smoothly, except that they hadn't been able to take out the whole tumor.

"Which means?"

I saw that he wasn't used to this. His patients surely never interrupt him. My voice had sounded aggressive, involuntarily. His reply was a little curt. "The tumor is less well placed than we thought. It's complicated to remove the whole thing without risking serious tissue damage. We're dealing with a very fragile area, you understand?"

I understood, but I didn't like it. I mean, that wasn't the agreement. The previous day, the terms had been set out clearly: they would remove the entire tumor. I had said yes, I'd turned over my son to him, and he'd split him in half. Did he realize?

Of course, I said all that to myself. The surgeon hemmed and hawed. He'd been able to extract a significant portion of the tumor, and that was the most important thing. Pierre needed rest. He was going to have some more tests, and then they'd decide.

He paused. He stared at the door, looking impatient. Fear and panic took hold of me. Was I supposed to say something at this point? Maybe it was up to me to ask good questions.

In the end, he stood up straight and consulted his watch. "What can she be doing? We said one o'clock..."

He wasn't talking to me; I didn't ask for clarification. I looked at the door and understood that clarity would come from there. I didn't know what it would be—and moreover, I didn't want to know. I wasn't ready. I stared at that door and prayed it wouldn't open. Ever.

I felt a sudden urge to throw myself at it. To hold it shut, to break the handle that shone against the white background. It was stupid, but as long as that door stayed shut, everything remained possible. I mean, out in the corridor, there was still uncertainty. All conceivable futures were there, dancing on the other side of the door. A crowd of eventualities with their probabilities. Yes, as long as no one opened the door, reality remained free: it could head in any direction at all. Parallel worlds. I could see them distinctly, the beautiful ones, and then others a bit uglier. It was normal; balance is necessary everywhere. No, what counts is hope. One word too many, one expression, or one opening door—and the conditional is dead.

If only the handle wouldn't move. If only the door would remain closed forever.

Obviously, the hospital didn't see things the same way. There was a sick man, and there was his father, waiting for him. There was the truth. Physicians are rational people.

A woman came in. A brunette in her early forties. Little round eyeglasses, perched halfway down her nose. She shook my hand. "Hello, I'm Dr. Ward, the oncologist. I apologize for being late—I was with another patient."

I didn't react right away. The surgeon most probably thought I hadn't understood. "She's a cancer specialist," he explained.

I blinked. I was just in time to see the futures breaking apart on the horizon.

She told me there would be other tests. She was pessimistic about the diagnosis. "It's pancreatic cancer." The cells were metastasizing, and there was a risk of propagation. "We're going to have to discuss what treatments to consider."

The surgeon wished me "Good luck for the rest" and slipped away.

"Don't worry, I'll be in charge from here on," his colleague reassured me. "We're going to take good care of your son."

She gazed at me steadily, and I wasn't sure where I should aim my eyes. A nurse came in to announce that another patient had woken up. Dr. Ward made a sign with her hand, and the young woman went out without closing the door again.

"We'll talk about all this again with Pierre. You can mention it to him, but don't feel obligated. I'll be there to accompany you. Don't hesitate to ask us for help."

She was smiling. I had trouble understanding her last words. I said "Thanks," but that wasn't what I was thinking.

You do what you can with your lips.

They brought Pierre back to me at one o'clock sharp. He seemed conscious but completely lost. They explained that he was still under the effects of the anesthetic. "He'll snap out of it in the afternoon."

I stayed by his side. He opened his eyes from time to time. When his eyelids fluttered, my whole chest tightened. "Pierre? Say something. Anything at all."

I spoke to him several times without success. He had to wake up soon, I thought, because I could see him stirring. He was in pain. His forehead betrayed the signs of a desperate struggle. He was trying to turn over, but a groan escaped him with every movement. It killed me to see him like that, pinned down on his back, I could tell it was bothering him. I wanted to act, but I had no idea of what I ought to do. Once again, I felt terribly powerless. I prayed that it wouldn't become a habit. Finally, a nurse looked in and changed his IV bag.

He came to an hour later. With his eyes on me, which made me feel good. I smiled at him and asked how he was doing. He made a face. I said, stupidly, that his discomfort would go away, and I put my hand on his forehead. It relieved me to see him wake up. It was as if my guts untangled themselves under my navel.

I thought back to what the oncologist had said. The cancer, the treatments. How could I have the slightest discussion with him now? He fell asleep again, and I slumped in my chair. Sleep was invading every cell in my brain. I closed my eyes and let it come.

The oncologist came back toward the end of the afternoon. She nodded to me in greeting and woke up Pierre. She asked some questions. As he repeated that he was hurting, she promised to increase his dosage of painkillers.

I was on the sidelines, feeling insignificant. My mouth was furry from my nap, and I cast my eyes around for a bottle of water. While the doctor gave us some details about the operation, I saw Pierre try to sit up straight in his bed. She spoke clearly and slowly. Pierre didn't look as though he understood her very well; I saw him nodding his head mechanically. His features grew more and more tense. I wondered why she didn't run off and find something to make him feel better.

As soon as she left the room, he closed his eyes. I could tell he was concentrating on his pain; I was sorry I wasn't suffering too. I waited a little while, and then I stepped out into the corridor. A nurse was busying herself around a cart. She was in her thirties, a blonde with her hair pulled back. I didn't like making a fuss, but Pierre was hurting too much. I explained that as well as I could. I thought she was going to get annoyed, but she smiled and said, "I'll be there right away."

11

Of course, there's only one doubt. I've often wondered whether I was the only person it occurred to. Could her parents have considered it as well? I'll never know.

It didn't come all at once. In the beginning, when they called me, I didn't realize. Lucille, car crash, tree. At first, shock dominates everything else. It takes over your brain, and your heart starts beating hard.

"No...no...no..."

That's what I said, for sure. With my head wedged between my hands. Squatting down, my back flat against a cold wall. But in fact, I don't remember.

Everything went too fast the first few days. There was Pierre to take care of. I did a lot of running around, without really understanding. I didn't have a single moment to myself.

My memory of the funeral isn't very clear. Some silhouettes, some overlong silences. I remember being surprised to see all those people crowded around the coffin. With her illness, Lucille had cut herself off from the world. Many former friends had turned their backs on her, but death surely smooths over everything. The dead are all good people, as someone sang.

There were speeches I didn't listen to. I felt François's hand on my shoulder. I was glad to have him with me. I was sobbing like a child. I'd lost the love of my life, and that's like dying a little yourself.

I pulled myself together quickly. There was my son. It was terrible for him too, but he didn't realize that. In any case, growing up without a mother is an awful thing. Maybe that was the reason why I became so close to him. Was I trying to compensate for his loss? I have no idea.

The inquest was what plunged me into the thing. Or maybe it was just that by then I'd had time to reflect. There was a witness; he said that the car had been going too fast. It had gone into a skid and left the road.

Lucille detested speeding.

Later, they told me she hadn't been wearing her seatbelt, and I didn't believe them. That wouldn't have been at all like her. They were positive, so then I thought she was probably under the influence of some of her pills. The experts assured me she wasn't.

A police captain curtly announced his conclusion, namely that the crash was "a stupid accident, the kind that happens often." I had a ton of questions, which I failed to ask. I felt like an idiot. They weren't needed anymore.

I've never talked about this before. Is it important? Well, it continues to haunt *me*. Always this feeling of helplessness, this sense that I could die of guilt. Pierre knows only the official version. I don't want him asking the same questions as me.

I don't often speak to him about his mother. It's not that I refuse, it's just that I'm not sure what story to tell him. There's a love story, of course, but that's none of his business. As for the rest, I've never been capable of putting it into words.

12

This evening I had a rendezvous with François. There's a bar we sometimes meet in. It's a little bistro on a narrow street not far from the main square. It's a practical choice, because it stays open all night. Drivers often go there for a break, and also lots of other guys. I think they don't have any better places to go to. Sometimes men turn up angry because they've got themselves kicked out of their houses. They drink two-three beers, grumbling all the while, and then, once they've calmed down, they leave.

On the weekends, random groups of young people descend on the bar. They're already drunk, and they've come to prolong the party. Not very interesting. We meet there only on weekdays, often in the middle of the night. We drink coffee or beer, depending on the mood and the hour. The place is a bit small, but we always find a table. I don't like sitting at the counter, it makes me feel like my conversation's being overheard. And besides, you look like a drunk, sitting there with your elbows on the bar.

When I came in, I saw François sitting in the back. He was waiting for me with a double espresso on the table in front of him—alcohol is for after the shift's over. I looked at my watch: it was two o'clock in the morning, an early time to take a break. I told myself I'd go back to work after this little pause. In any case, I had nothing better to do. When I'm working, I forget the rest for a little while.

I'd seen François on the day after the operation. I'd told him about the pancreatic cancer. At the word "cancer," I'd watched his face tense up.

When he saw me coming toward him, he got to his feet. He held my shoulder and shook my hand. He does that every time; he says it's more ceremonious, government ministers do it on TV, and there's no reason not to imitate them. I think he does it mostly because it amuses him. François has always loved playing the clown. That's doubtless the reason why I appreciate him so much.

I sat down and asked for a beer. I could see his surprise, but he made no comment. That was good. I had no desire to justify myself. I wanted a beer, so that's what I ordered.

"Well, have you had a lot of fares?"

I took a sip of the lager the waiter had placed in front of me. I shook my head no, and he sighed. "Yeah, same with me. The weather's too nice. People are walking or riding bikes."

I hadn't paid much attention to the temperature. François is always looking for explanations. What makes a guy raise his arm when he sees us passing by? Why do

certain nights go better than others? I don't think there
are reasons for everything.

"One more bad night..."

He'd picked up a couple. Thirty years old at the most,
both of them. They'd spent the whole ride fighting with
each other.

"Especially the girl. Did she do some yelling at him!
I could tell he was embarrassed. He kept giving me little
headshakes. But look, he didn't just sit there and take it
either. You wouldn't believe the way he answered her!"

François interrupted himself to finish his coffee and
then took up where he'd left off: "So, they were yelling and
yelling. They had even totally forgotten I was there! She
hollered that she was going to get out—I believe she was
half crying—and he went her one better. He told her, very
distinctly, to go fuck herself. And then they started over
again. And again, and again. The tension kept mounting,
I was sure they would come to blows any second..."

I sighed and nodded, because that sort of thing happened to me too. I never dared to tell my passengers to get
out of my taxi. I asked him, "So what did you do?"

"Me? Oh, nothing. We still had a ways to go, I was
afraid the babe would tell me to stop. You understand. I
didn't want to give up on the fare..."

"Yeah..."

"To tell you the truth, they didn't bother me. I couldn't
say why, but I didn't think it was serious. Funny, huh?
They're just about to start duking it out, and I'm up there

thinking they look like they're crazy in love." He scratched his head. "What could have made me think that? I don't know. Instinct, no doubt. Maybe after seeing so many people pass in and out of my cab…"

As I listened to his tale, I remembered Lucille telling me once that we were "the privileged witnesses of the human condition."

"Basically," François went on, "that was just an impression. I mean, it's simply my vision of them. I told myself, 'They love each other,' but maybe they were hardly out of the car before they broke up for good…Go figure. Every time you take on a fare, you imagine a whole bunch of things. You pick up a guy, you two chat a little, and you say to yourself, 'This guy must be a good family man, a good father.' But then he goes home, and for all you know, he beats his kids and he rapes his wife! It's always the same. Well, yes, sure, the real pricks, you learn to see them coming. But sometimes I tell myself that my taxi is a world all its own. A kind of magic box, you know?"

"It's true that your cab's looking more and more like a box…"

"Stop being an asshole, that's not what I mean."

I looked at François. He was staring at the empty cup in front of him.

"That's what I find most frustrating," he added, pinching his lip. "It's frustrating because all you get are tiny chunks of life. You judge people on the basis of so little...Even with all my experience, when I watch my passengers leave, I can't help wondering whether I'm wrong about them. All you have is what you see."

I had felt that before myself. The people in the back seat of my cab, I don't pretend to understand their lives, and so I try to guess. Which is certainly not much of an achievement, I know, but it seems just about as accurate as anything else.

François had fallen silent. He was eyeing my beer enviously.

"I went to see Pierre in the hospital," I said softly.

He raised his eyes. "How's he doing?"

I sighed. It was hard for me to find my words.

"All right...He's gradually recovering from the operation. I'd like for the treatment to start, but the folks at the hospital say he's still too weak. I—I don't know. I think the sooner they get started, the better it is, no?"

François hesitated. "Uh...yes, yes. Absolutely. But then, you have to trust the doctors. They're the ones who know what's best for Pierre."

"The doctors. You know, I don't often see doctors. Mostly it's nurses. They've very nice, but they can't really answer my questions. The oncologist comes in in the morning, I think. I've only seen her once."

"The oncologist?"

"A cancer specialist. Pierre's her patient."

He whistled between his teeth. He didn't like hearing the word "cancer." At some point, I thought I'd understood him to suggest that his father had died of it.

"Don't worry, Yanis. They're going to cure your son for you." As he said that, he planted his eyes deep in mine.

"Yes," I said, grimacing, and then I finished my beer.

13

I hardly sleep anymore. I can't stand waiting for the day, so I work until morning. At ten o'clock, I drop off my last fare, and then I come to the hospital. I've been starting to go back on duty earlier and earlier, sometimes right after I leave Pierre.

In the beginning, I was surprised. I thought things would get complicated, I wouldn't be able to keep it up. But as it turns out, it's not so hard. I can't close my eyes anymore. I'm tired, of course, but that's different—lying down wouldn't change a thing. And obviously, there's a price to pay: I'm pale, and I've lost weight. François often points this out to me.

This morning, I knew from the moment I entered the room that today would be different. Maybe it was the look in Pierre's eyes, which were brighter and more determined. Or maybe something else, something in the atmosphere. It's difficult to explain.

I sat beside him. He stared at me like I was a halluci-
nation. His chemotherapy medication is so strong it wears
him out. He spends half his time lost in a fog I can't pull
him out of. It breaks me down to see him like that.

Gemcitabine, once a week, in an infusion that lasts for
half an hour. I watched the liquid running down into his
veins. Into my son's blood. A terrible molecule, a lethal
agent charged with eliminating undesirable cells. A poison. "A good poison," as a nurse once said to correct me.

He hadn't lost his hair. That surprised me. That was
all I knew about chemotherapy: you go bald. Obviously,
it's more complicated than that; but me, I'm no specialist. Cancer and I had never met. The word scared me, it
scares everybody, but its echo was too far away. A muffled
threat, a vague danger. Like the thermonuclear bomb or
a nasty hernia.

"I tried to work."

I didn't grasp his meaning right away. He'd sat up a
little as he spoke. I said nothing, waiting for him to go on.

"It's . . . it's hard. You know, I have trouble concentrating because of the . . . the medicine . . . I'm so tired."

I felt my stomach tighten. I was afraid. The week before, we'd clashed over the subject of his treatment. He
wanted to cut back on it—the chemo made him vomit.
He was suffering from diarrhea and losing weight. "My

friends don't recognize me anymore! I can see it in their eyes..."

He'd tossed that at me as if it was my fault. I remember the frustration I'd felt. The injustice, too.

So then I'd started yelling. It was ugly and I was ashamed of myself, but he had to understand. The medicine would save his life. I shouted that at him with all my might. I also screamed that he was young, and that it was fortunate that he was young. That the doctors had told me so. And that he would get well, because we would try everything. I'd ask for the heaviest drugs, I said. Even experimental ones. He was in good shape, he could take it. He'd stick it out. Getting well was mostly mental. And he'd be well advised to fight, because I was bound and determined to bring him back.

I had yelled all that at him, standing above his bed, my eyes drowned in tears. It was strange, because he was crying too. He bleated, "Okay, Dad, okay! Okay!" But I couldn't stop. I needed to be sure, to drive my point home. So that he'd never again ask to back off his treatment.

That's why I was afraid. Listening to him talk that way... I didn't even feel strong enough to get worked up.

I didn't answer. He leaned forward to pick up a folder from his night table. "It's my book," he said. "I've finished it, I think."

I felt heat surging through my chest. Relief, and happiness too. Seeing him go back to his projects—that was unexpected. I asked if I could read it, and he smiled and handed me the manuscript, saying, "Yes, of course."

Then he hesitated a moment, choosing his words. I gave him an encouraging look.

"I'd like you to send it to some editors."

I took the folder and opened it. It contained a stack of pages covered with lines. On the first sheet, the title appeared in capital letters. And just below it: "Pierre Marès."

I said I couldn't wait to start reading it. Hoping to please him, I spoke about his theater piece. A hint of sadness crossed his face. I apologized, but it was too late. Beyond those walls, life was continuing on its way. Without him. And I'd just reminded him of that.

To change the subject, I asked him for some details. I wanted to know about this pitch to the editors. He told me I should start by copying the manuscript. I was supposed to send it out just about everywhere; he'd prepared a letter to accompany it.

I had trouble grasping everything. The idea upset me, but I wasn't able to articulate why. I knew nothing about such things, but it seemed to me that a first draft wasn't enough. Wouldn't it be better to wait? Surely there would be some corrections to make, some details or outside opinions to consider.

That impatience bothered me. It wasn't like him.

All the same, when I left him, I promised I'd try to do what he wanted. Did I have a choice? He was right, no doubt. It was his thing, his passion. Surely he knew what was best.

I had the folder under my arm. In the corridor, two nurses were bustling around the doorway to a room. I asked if Dr. Ward was there. They answered that she was scheduled to drop by the unit and suggested that I take a seat in the waiting room. A young woman who was sitting in there greeted me as I entered. She was tall and dark-haired; she looked like she might be a foreigner, but I wasn't sure. Her black hair was tied up; a few escaped strands fell down to her shoulders. She was beautiful, almost intimidating.

She was looking through the window at the parking lot. Her face was serious, dignified, and yet very sweet. Her eyes looked red to me. I didn't dare stare at her, so I settled for quick glances. She was young, not yet thirty. I told myself that she was like Pierre, she had no business being here. I tried to imagine her outside, happy, laughing. Yes, that was better. I often made the same effort for my son. The idea was to get him out of his room. There was still life out there beyond those white walls. It was reassuring to keep repeating that.

I wanted to go and sit beside her. Maybe someone ought to tell her, I thought. Misfortune wasn't everything; it would be enough to whisper that to her. I couldn't, of course. Maybe there was a time when I could have, back when Lucille was around. What had made me change so much? I was nothing but a coward anymore. That's growing old, I guess.

A nurse tapped on the door and announced, "He's ready. You can go in."

The young woman nodded slowly and followed the nurse. I remained alone, wedged into my chair with some stupid regrets.

An *hour passed*, maybe more. Everything's too long here; that's what it's like in places where you don't want to be.

"You wanted to see me?"

The oncologist had come in. I had an urge to speak to her about my long wait, but I didn't dare. She stayed on her feet, so I stood up too. We were face to face, and I realized she was barely shorter than me.

I asked her about Pierre's chemotherapy. I wanted to know how far along it was. I didn't understand why he hadn't shown any improvement. "When am I going to be able to bring him home?" I asked. "He's been here nearly a month!"

She hesitated—it took her several seconds to respond to me. I imagine she was weighing her words.

She told me that the situation was more complicated. The operation had weakened Pierre. He was taking little nourishment and not sleeping well. "Right now he's affected as much by the treatment as by the disease."

It wasn't possible for him to leave the hospital anytime soon. Not desirable, either. "Not for him, not for you."

So when, then?

I lost my temper. Was anyone finally going to tell me what I could expect next? They were physicians, surely they had some ideas in their heads. Some leads, at least, some percentages, some statistics, stuff like that. How did things go in other, similar cases? "Listen," I said. "I just want to know when he's going to recover."

She lowered her eyes. Not long, a fraction of a second.

"I'm sorry, Mr. Marès. In your son's case, we can't really talk about a recovery."

I took the blow without trembling and without loosening my lips. The violence of the shock. I hadn't realized. Or then again, yes, I knew already. Yes, that was it. A vague specter, an icy breath. A truth that had been following me everywhere. It was there, crouched behind me, hidden in my shadow. I had just turned around to look it in the face.

The oncologist gave me the best explanation she could. She was sincere, I could feel it. There were no more things unsaid, no more innuendos. It was too late for them now. She told me that chemotherapy made it possible to slow down the evolution of the disease, in some cases even to stop it. They were trying to gain as much time as possible. And it could be a lot, after all. Some people live for decades with cancer. But there was one thing I had to understand: there was no recovering from a metastasized tumor.

I was planted on my two legs. I tried to drive them into the floor. I was afraid I'd start shaking; I couldn't have people thinking I wasn't up to the ordeal.

I asked, "Does Pierre know this?"

She nodded. "He's assimilating it, little by little. Accepting the disease takes time. A psychologist has been working with him. He hasn't told you?"

"No," I mumbled. Then I thanked her and went out. In the corridor, I tried to keep my head high. Pierre's folder was still clamped under my arm. I squeezed it as hard as I could.

PART TWO

1

In *the past few days*, I've received three negative responses. Form letters, no explanations. Just "No," accompanied by a few polite phrases. I wasn't surprised; I'm waiting
for the others, the responses to the rest of my twenty-five
submissions. It's already been a month. Is so much time really required? Yesterday, a journalist I was driving to the
train station tried to give me an explanation. According to
him, there are too many manuscripts. The waiting time is
long because people send in any old rubbish.

In the hospital, Pierre checks for updates every morning. I haven't been able to tell him about the rejections.

I dropped by to see him today. He was in a bad mood. I
felt his frustration vibrating in the silences, like a seething
liquid. No matter how hard I tried, I couldn't get him to
unclench his teeth. At one point, I sat down right next
to him. I felt like taking his hand, but I didn't dare. He
was white, with dark circles around his eyes. A lump was
climbing up my throat. I wanted to help him; there was

nothing I wouldn't have done. I had the impression that he was slipping away between my fingers. I tried to make eye contact with him, but it was becoming too hard. So I left the room.

In the corridor, a nurse came up to me.

"Sir, is everything all right?"

I couldn't bring myself to answer her.

"I'm Rosalie. I often take care of your son."

I thanked her. She was young; I wondered if she was the same age as Pierre. Probably not. It wasn't very important.

"You're leaving already?"

I muttered that I'd be back. "In the afternoon," I said.

I wasn't proud. Did she think I was abandoning my son? I murmured that he didn't want to see me, that he was too tired.

"From working on his book?"

I must have recoiled, because she caught me by the arm. She told me not to worry. Pierre talked constantly about his book, she said. Everybody on the staff knew about it.

"It's often that way with this type of disease. The patient gets fixated on something. It's a kind of self-defense. His brain turns away from his suffering."

I didn't reply, and she went on. "Sometimes the patient's family and friends complicate things. In your son's case, his manuscript fixation often tends to put him in a bad mood. But it's important. Even essential. It gives him a goal."

She smiled at me again.

"It's crucial, you see. It allows him to escape."

And again, I didn't know what to say. Escape. That sounded good.

One of her colleagues called her, and she made a sign that she was coming. But first she said to me, "Don't worry. Come back this afternoon, I'm sure he'll be doing better. And don't neglect this manuscript question. It's too important to him."

She walked a few steps away and then turned around and faced me again. "And besides, who knows? Maybe it'll be published one day!"

After I got back to the apartment, I looked over the addresses of the editors. They were all in Paris, all right in the heart of the capital—which didn't surprise me. I got back in my cab. There was a long way to go, but I drove without stopping. As I drove, I felt better and better. My hands lightly gripped the steering wheel as I ate up the kilometers. At last, I was doing something.

At the first editor's door, I rang the bell, but no one came to let me in. It was past noon. I didn't feel like waiting, so I consulted my list and chose a big name. One I'd already heard of. All the same, I was surprised to find myself in front of an entire building. The name was written everywhere on the facade—very impressive.

I was pretty low-key at reception: "I submitted a manuscript, and I'd like to find out about it."

The receptionist pursed his lips. "I'm sorry, but there's nothing I can do. You must be patient, we receive a great many manuscripts." He assured me that mine would be read and considered. "Very carefully," he specified.

I explained that my case was more complicated, but he was already losing patience. "Sir, there's no use insisting."

I felt it rising up in me. I didn't want it to. I asked him why they needed so much time. I said, "It's been a month!"

I didn't like my tone or the anger that had crept into it. The man spoke firmly: "Sir, I must ask you to be so kind as to leave."

A woman came in. She was wearing a pants suit over a white blouse with the sleeves rolled up to her elbows. I noticed the way the guy at the reception desk looked at her: she was somebody important.

That was when I panicked. I interrupted the receptionist fellow and started talking nonsense. The woman didn't understand a thing, you could read it on her face. I talked about Pierre and the hospital. She asked me if he was a character in my book. I said no, it was because of the cancer. She knit her brows. I couldn't believe it. The absurdity of the situation shattered me. It's hard to attend your own downfall. The words kept coming out, but they weren't mine anymore. Things were going from bad to worse.

Suddenly, I felt ashamed. It came all at once, a feeling of indescribable shame. I turned my back on them and ran away. I put a kilometer's worth of streets between them and me before I succeeded in stopping myself. Out of breath and empty of everything else, I sat on a bench. Nothing was left; there was no more anger and no more shame. I was simply worn out. Yes, that's it. Too worn out. An infinite weariness was spreading all the way to my limbs. I tore up the addresses. The bits of paper floated like confetti between my legs.

2

It took me some time to accept it. Condemned to not knowing. Understanding's a necessity; ignorance is a poison. But it was no doubt my fault.

The inquest didn't drag on. There was only one witness, and he had simply seen "a car going too fast and then striking a tree." Lucille hadn't said anything and hadn't left any sort of note. So what conclusions would you draw? Nobody could do anything about it anymore. I felt no resentment.

Whatever follows is in the realm of the imagination. Or of faith. Reasoning does no good, it never really works. Can you just stop your thought processes?

An accident. An accident. A terrible accident.

I repeated that about a thousand times. Just to smother fear and stave off guilt.

.   .   .

One day, François suggested it might have been a voluntary act. I answered sincerely: not possible, I said, I didn't believe it. Lucille was sick, but to go from there to ending it all…

So why, then? There's always this doubt. It hangs around, it's everywhere; it gnaws at me a little every day. I look for evidence that doesn't exist. And the same question keeps coming back, always, incessantly: was it my fault too?

The truth is, I have no idea. Basically, it will never really be an accident.

It won't ever be suicide, either.

Is there something in between the two?

3

Since Pierre's been in the hospital, I see more of François. Usually, he's the one who initiates the call. Seeing him does me good, even though it's complicated because my life's in such disarray. I don't feel much like doing anything anymore; I must be hard to bear.

I'm never up for going out, so François invites himself over to my apartment. He brings food. After the meal, he asks me if it's all right if he lights a cigarette. I say yes every time, but he keeps asking.

He went over to the window, and I heard him strike a match. His back was to me, and I saw the smoke rising into the night.

"How's Pierre doing?"

That surprised me. Ordinarily, he never brings up the subject himself. He waits for me, and I think I appreciate that.

I muttered something, and he shook his head. "Forgive me, Yanis... It's just that... you don't look so good today."

I lowered my eyes. It bothered me to know he was worried. I had an urge to tell him how much I loved him, but the words stayed stuck in my throat. Better so; it would have sounded a little ridiculous. I don't generally make that kind of declaration.

He lit another cigarette, and all of a sudden, I started to talk.

I told him the story of Pierre's book. I tried to keep calm as I explained it, but the words escaped me. It was strange; I no longer had control over my sentences. It was like listening to someone else talk. I wondered if I was going crazy.

I tried to shut up; my lips kept moving. I heard my voice; it came from far away. It rose in the living room, it bounced off the walls. It grew shrill here and there, as it will when I get upset; it was deafening.

I realized that this was the same as what had happened a little earlier, when I spoke to the editor in the white blouse. The independence of my mouth, while all the rest shirked. A bridge. From my heart to my tongue. A flood of words cresting in front of me. It was close to intolerable. Did he, François, really want to hear that?

As a matter of fact, it was too late. I was sorry, but there was nothing I could do. I'd lost my grip. The source was in some other location, namely my guts. There was a force in me that chose to overrule everything else. Reticence, reserve, all those things you impose on yourself—the force didn't want a damn thing to do with any of them. It was making my soul scream, and making me its victim too.

Then there was silence; I didn't dare raise my eyes. I didn't know how long I'd been talking. François was sitting in the armchair facing the sofa. A scent of tobacco wafted through the room. I saw his hands; he was playing with his wedding ring. He turned it around and around on his finger and then slid it up to the top joint. It was a beautiful ring, gold with reddish highlights. I'd never really noticed it before.

"Listen, Yanis…"

He was watching me, looking embarrassed. And hesitant. I sensed that he was holding his words back. There was a fight going on inside his skull.

"I don't know if this can help you, but I happen to know an editor. It's a small operation, they put out a few books a year, not very many. But anyway…I don't know…Maybe I could show her Pierre's book."

I had to make a huge effort to stay calm. Everything became blurry. My heart started beating fast, the rest of me seized up. François's eyes begged me not to get too excited. The seconds passed, I felt like dancing. I wanted to throw my arms around his neck, I wanted to hug him hard. Nothing at all had been gained as yet, but for the first time, I was being given a little hope. François was opening a door for me. Just barely, almost not at all; a sliver of light in the gap. It was like being tossed a little bitty life preserver: not much to cling to, but at least something.

Well, all the same, I held myself in check. Out of a sense of decency, and out of respect for him. I asked for some details in a detached tone that reassured him. He explained that his friend worked for a young publishing house. He offered to send her the manuscript. "That way you can be sure it'll get read." He stared at me for a long time before murmuring, "And after all, if they like it…"

He didn't finish his sentence. I didn't insist. I think that if I had been in his place, I would have taken the same precautions.

Anyway, I went to get a bottle of whiskey. I had some good stuff, a twenty-year-old scotch I kept on hand for special occasions. The bottle was three-quarters full, and I told myself that my life lacked occasions. Maybe I'm too demanding.

It's basically true that you should never wait. All those things you save for later—it's a heavy blow to die without having enjoyed them.

4

I arrived early for my appointment. The weather was fine, so I chose to pass the time by strolling along the river. The river walk in the city center is magnificent. The buildings remind us of our insignificance. I felt hotter and hotter, and then I started shivering. It was hard for me not to think about Pierre.

I stopped in front of a plaque. *To the memory of the thousands of children deported to the camps during the war.* I thought about all those dead kids. Thinking about them had no effect on me.

I retraced my steps. I felt bad, but I was trying not to let it show. I was afraid of what would happen with the editor. When you play your last card, you shut up and wait. I kept telling myself it would be over soon. Maybe I'd be buying a round somewhere later on.

I stepped into the restaurant, and the place made me feel better. The warmth of the dining room, the inevitable exposed beams, the wooden tables and chairs. Paintings decorated the walls; a yellow submarine hung behind the bar. The pictures were for sale. Little white labels dangled below the frames.

I gave the name of the reservation. At the table, I was relieved to see that only three places were set. There would be no surprise, no witness.

I ordered a glass of white.

"A chablis?"

I said yes. I would have said yes to anything at all.

I waited three glasses. The time didn't pass; I played with a corner of my napkin. I don't believe I thought about anything. Pierre says it's not possible to wait without thinking. I disagree.

They finally came in. François shook my hand and introduced me to his editor friend. I had pictured a tall, thin woman with straight hair, a little cold; she was short, round, curly-haired, and radiant. From behind her glasses, her eyes analyzed me. She said she was delighted. I thought she had the look of a former hippie.

François glanced at my empty glass and ordered a bottle. We sat down, and he asked me how I was doing. I said, "Fine." I've always found that an uninteresting question.

He got the conversation going and let the editor talk. She was really amusing; when she smiled, pretty dimples showed in her cheeks. In other circumstances, I would surely have appreciated her.

She described the world of publishing to me. One manuscript out of a thousand selected—a big lottery. The numbers she mentioned made my head spin. She continued by explaining that once books were published, there was often a lot of disappointment in store for the authors. "It's rare that good sales follow."

I hesitated. Nevertheless, I heard myself ask, "And what about Pierre?" Her face tensed. For barely a second, but I understood.

I tried to listen to what she was saying. Some of it was good, and I wanted to be able to repeat it to my son. His manuscript wasn't bad, it contained some fine passages; but they weren't enough. The structure was too weak, the ending too long.

"Maybe with more work..."

Her voice trailed off. She apologized with her eyes, and I made a sign that everything was all right.

I can't remember the rest of the meal. It was torture for her too. Playing the role of the good pal, François carried the conversation. I don't know whether I talked. Maybe to add one or two banalities. I thanked the editor when she left, because I didn't want her to feel guilty.

François ordered two cognacs. He stared at the table and said nothing.

"I can't do it."

Taken aback, he raised his eyes to look at me. "What do you mean, you can't do it?"

I had an urge to cry. A terribly strong urge. Some incredible thing rose up inside my chest. I couldn't take any more. It had to come out. It was awful that it had to fall on François, but maybe it was better so.

I explained that I couldn't tell Pierre it was all over, his manuscript would never be published; I couldn't tell him that he might die and that I, his father, was incapable of doing or changing anything about it. Besides, I said, I didn't want him to die. There was no reason for it, it wasn't fair. After all, I said, it could be me, or François, or the amusing editor. So then yes, why Pierre? Why my son, huh? No, really, I didn't understand. Besides, since his book wouldn't be published, there wasn't any reason for him to die anymore. He had every right to compose a second book. After all, other writers could write as many as they wanted. And anyway, fuck fucking writers and their fucking editors, and fuck him too, François, my good buddy, who couldn't be bothered to find me an understanding editor. Because it was true. What was all that shit about the thousands of manuscripts they've rejected? Me, I was concerned with only one. To them, that couldn't be such a big deal.

I noticed that the other diners in the restaurant were looking at us. I didn't give a shit, but I was embarrassed for François. I picked up my cognac glass and drained it in one gulp. It burned my throat.

I went out into the night and walked around aimlessly. I'd left François without another word. I saw a tobacco shop and went in to buy a pack of cigarettes. I hadn't smoked for the past twenty years. I'd stopped cold when my son was born. It wasn't so much for my own sake; I'd heard a report on the radio about secondhand smoke.

The tobacconist wouldn't accept a credit card payment for less than fifteen euros. That irritated me, and I told him so. I bought three packs and left two on the counter. Pretty cool move, I thought. I heard "Fucking asshole" as I went out, but I didn't turn around.

I didn't have a lighter. I couldn't see myself going back to the tobacco shop, so I waited for someone to come along. It was a Tuesday evening, but that's the advantage of cities: you're never completely alone. A pretty mixed-race girl offered me her lighter. I had a hard time because of the wind. I finally got my cigarette lit and gave her back her lighter, coughing as I did so. She smiled but didn't dare laugh.

Two drags later, my head was already spinning. I forced myself to take another drag, and another. It burned, but that was nothing compared to Pierre. I drew on the cigarette with all my might and triggered a coughing fit that bent me in half. The cigarette fell out of my hand. I pulled out the pack and threw it on the ground. A homeless person appeared out of a doorway. I took a step back. He shrugged and went to pick up the cigarettes. When he saw that the pack was nearly full, he looked at me contemptuously before hurrying away.

I trudged all the way to the waterfront. I went down the stairs and walked along the river. A few bums were joyfully knocking back the contents of their bottles. I sat some distance away from them, leaning forward over the water, my elbows jammed into my thighs.

The riverbanks are even more beautiful at night. The buildings glitter on the surface of the water; it's like looking at the stars with your head down. I realized I was crying when I saw my tears puncture the sky.

I thought about Pierre, about his disappointment. I told myself that I'd failed, that there was nothing to be done anymore. There were still two or three names on my list, but I had finally caught on. The amusing editor had done her job well. Pierre wouldn't publish. Pierre would never publish.

I was hurting myself, as I needed to do. I had an urge to press harder, the way you press on a wound. Just for the sight of blood. Had I missed something? Parents are supposed to be able to hang the moon.

I heard a cry. I turned my head but didn't see anything. Maybe it had come from farther away, from the shadows of a bridge. I doubted it. I must have been dreaming. In any case, the humming in my ears was too loud. I could feel my temples throbbing. I wanted to plunge back into my reverie, but I couldn't anymore. The cry had come from me. The wind was sliding down the back of my neck.

I could hear the world calling me to order.

5

I got no smile from Pierre when I entered his room. I found him pale—in fact, frighteningly white. I tried to engage him in conversation. I asked how his evening had been, and he replied that he didn't know, he couldn't tell the difference anymore. "Day, night, same thing." He appeared tense, exhausted. All the same, he eventually revealed that he'd watched a movie. "I didn't make it to the end," he said.

There was a silence. I knew his chemo altered his concentration. He couldn't read for very long either.

I sat in the armchair next to him. I was surprised that he said nothing about the book. I hesitated—maybe he would just give up the idea. He'd kept his eyes fixed on the window since I came in.

"You should go."

That took my breath away. The hardness in his voice, the effort he was making to hurt me. I knew he was mad at me, and I felt like encouraging him. I would take it on, his pain; I'd take it on with pleasure, even. If that could relieve him. Me too, I knew how to suffer. To be with him, or in his place.

He wouldn't look at me. I felt the tears welling up and left the room. In the corridor, I leaned my head against the wall. Blood was rushing to my temples; I had to let my emotions calm down. I felt like vomiting and headed for the restroom. No one was in there. I went into a stall and took the time to latch the door before kneeling. Nothing came up. I stuck a finger down my throat. Once, twice. The third time, I felt my stomach turn. I vomited coffee. It was black, I was surprised to see I'd drunk so much. I tried again but brought up only bile, which burned my throat.

Someone came in. I wiped my mouth and flushed the toilet. I was afraid of being too red, afraid of being conspicuous. I took a deep breath. The guy went into the stall next to mine.

Standing in front of the mirror, I saw a white, exhausted face.

Back in the corridor, I spotted the oncologist. When she saw me, she interrupted her discussion and came to speak to me. The stairway was between us. I wanted to walk faster and flee up the stairs. My legs refused.

"Mr. Marès?"

I took her hand. She smiled politely. She'd looked in on Pierre, but I'd been out of the room. She wanted to talk to me. "Can I offer you some coffee in my office?" I thought back on the puke in the toilet. An opaque black. I said yes, and she smiled again.

Her office was located in the other wing. The place was a cubbyhole, practically at the dead end of a corridor. Impressed as I had been by her, she lost her loftiness by receiving me there. There was a table with a computer on it and barely enough room left over for a notebook. Two chairs faced each other.

The walls were entirely bare. No painting, no photograph. I inspected the table: not the smallest picture of her children. When I made that observation, she blinked. "I don't have any." She explained that she shared the space with another specialist. I thought back to a TV report I'd seen on the hospital. I'd changed the channel, because I found it ridiculous to feel sorry for physicians.

She asked me how I liked my coffee. I didn't react right away. "You don't want coffee anymore?"

Then I refocused and said, "Yes, yes. Black, no sugar."

I didn't know where to look. There was a glass wall behind her, with a pivot window in its upper part. The window was fixed to a metal rod, but even opened as far as it would go, there was barely enough space to admit a breath of fresh air. I found that depressing, and I wondered why people installed such systems. Below the window, a gray filing cabinet blocked a significant portion of the light.

She put a plastic cup in front of me and sat down. She tapped on her computer and furrowed her brow as she read her notes—a real doctorly trick. Finally, she looked up at me. She had green, magnificent eyes. They gazed deeply into mine.

"Pierre's condition has worsened."

"Yes, I can see that."

She went into detail. The cancer was spreading. "It's extremely painful. The disease is attacking his liver and lungs as well. The cells have metastasized. He's on morphine at the moment—we'll see if his condition stabilizes."

I had a headache. It was hot, the office was too small. You can't talk cancer in a closet. I took a sip of coffee. My blurred gaze wandered over her shoulders. The window was still behind her. I closed my eyes.

Fathers are the reason hospitals hire security.

She took a long, deep breath. I stiffened. I saw that she regretted her unguarded reaction at once. I'd understood, and it was too late: now I was on my guard.

"Mr. Marès."

Her voice was a murmur, soft and somehow comforting.

"There's something you really must understand."

I agreed, as if to say I was ready to hear it.

"Your son is now in palliative care. We've stopped his treatments; it's time to keep him comfortable and free from pain."

I said, repeating her, "You've stopped his treatments."

Still her green eyes, wedged between mine.

"It's so we can support him along the way, you understand? So we can maintain his quality of life, as much as possible."

I said yes, I understood. I wasn't lying. I understood. I could tell from the pain in my chest. I understood.

A cold anger rose up in me; I hadn't seen it coming. I got worked up. Maintain his quality of life. What did that mean? My son's quality of life was what, exactly? I didn't get it. What was it that had to be maintained? Did he still have a life? With that monster in his innards, that thing devouring him from inside? Every day, I watched him fade away a little more. My son, helplessly bedridden, dopey from his medications. And doomed to boot?

What were they going to maintain the quality of if he was already dead?

She lowered her eyes. "I'm very sorry."

Me, I'd had it with all these sorry people. I didn't want them to be sorry. I didn't want them to maintain his quality of life. I wanted them to maintain his *life*. Quality could come later. And besides, that part was my responsibility. I'd be able to take care of his quality. But first they had to give him back to me, they had to do their damn job. Anyway, it was nuts, the whole thing was nuts. And besides, who'd made the decision to stop his treatments?

She told me to calm down. I would have liked her to bawl me out, but she spoke very kindly to me. That was worse, and it made me ashamed. I got up. I heard her say, "Come back and see me when you're feeling better." I walked to the elevator. Hot blood rose to my head and stung my cheeks.

His quality of life.

And me? What had I done for his quality of life? I recalled Pierre's unsmiling face. His eyes, shouting at me to help him. The look of a son abandoned by his father. His quality of life.

The elevator doors opened, but I didn't move. Behind me, a nurse asked, "Aren't you getting in?" I turned around.

I retraced my steps down the corridor. I had no more control of what I was doing. I reached the door of Pierre's room and went in without knocking. He was dozing. I sat down beside the bed and took his hand.

"Pierre?"

He opened his eyes. With an effort. I don't know whether he recognized me. All the same, he sat up a little after a few seconds.

"It's Dad. Can you hear me, Pierre?"

He nodded. I leaned over him and murmured, "An editor called."

6

I didn't go to see him today. Didn't have the nerve. Then again, it may have been something else: didn't feel like it. Maybe I was mad at him too.

I got on the road and drove to the coast. I was thinking about my son, and it was like an ache in my guts. Was it possible to forget him? Or even better, should I have never had him? Yes, I liked that idea. Alone, I would have had a chance. When I loved people, they wrecked me. First Lucille, and now Pierre. In the long run, if you never love anybody, you spare yourself.

All that thinking distracted me, and meanwhile the accelerator pedal was crushed against the floor. I was drifting, slipping away, far from the world. I was so sick and tired of being that guy, that half of a man, devastated with fear and grief. And then there was the guilt I felt, a never-ending thing. It had to stop. Sure, I'd told a lie, but it wasn't my fault. I'd been forced, I had no choice. Pierre, his eyes, his suffering, plastered all over like a poster. No one had given me anything, not the least bit of hope. Futures taken and ruined, right before my eyes. Whole lives, suddenly gone. Not just Pierre's, but mine too. And Lucille's.

I drove on, and the pain spread out. Like a wave, all the way to my fingertips, but still less violent somehow. I wanted everything to stop. Suppose I closed my eyes. It would be simple, all I'd have to do was wait. The slow deviation from a straight trajectory. To break out at last, to leave the goddamned road laid out for me. There would be an impact: violent, muffled, immediate. And, with a little luck, irreparable.

I gave it some thought and saw it was cowardly, and I was already such a coward. After all, dying was clearly the easiest way out.

I didn't close my eyes. I felt like diving. Holding my breath and plunging underwater—I missed doing that. The tranquillity of it was something I'd never found anywhere else. I gripped the steering wheel tight and told myself that if I concentrated, I could make the weight inside my chest disappear.

When I parked at the beach, my heartbeat slowed down. After putting on my gear, I did some stretching. Then I stared out at the sea, and it was self-evident.

In fact, I don't remember ever dreaming about anything else. I mean, when I was a kid, I already had the itch. All I had to do was fix my eyes on the surface. Just to imagine its depths, nothing but that, was intoxicating. And then farther off, of course, beyond the horizon. Often, when the sea was calm, I would wait, standing up, arms at my sides, my ears pricked. That was how I learned to see it coming. A little wind, and everything would start moving. It always began the same way: a wrinkle on the surface, a flag twitching at the entrance to the harbor. I've always loved that slow movement of great masses, the old motor coughing before turning over. The waves would surge toward me, and it fascinated me to know that they came from the other side of the world.

Lucille loved that too. We'd sit on the rocks, the two of us, just to look. Like you do in front of a fire, without saying a word. With your eyes pointed at the dancing flames. Sometimes she'd press herself against me and I could hear her breathing. Her heart would be beating too fast. That would worry me, but I didn't say anything. My Lucille—I don't think she would have been able to dive with us.

I slipped into the water and felt the cold run underneath my wetsuit. Soon I'd get warm, but first there's a period of transition. I looked down and swam a few flat-palm strokes to get away from the shallows. The waves near the shore stirred up too much sand.

When I reached the rocks, the water was seven meters deep. I pushed out a little farther. I swam for almost half an hour; I couldn't see the bottom anymore. I dived three or four times, holding my breath for two minutes or so, nothing spectacular. It was pleasant to stop breathing. I loved the void around me; the silence, when the heart fades out.

As I rose to the surface, I felt a current pushing me out to sea. It wasn't very strong, and I amused myself by letting it have its way with me. In the end, I reached the surface. I blew into my snorkel to free it of water; I didn't want to thrust my head out into the air just yet. Because it's only when I'm submerged that I can relax. I mean, there's always something I have to think about. Problems, worries, there's no end to them. Sometimes they're just little things, it's true, and at other times they're a bit bigger. But I always think a person has to fight. And then I get tired. Besides, when is it, exactly, that you can pause to breathe? On Lucille's grave, they wrote REST IN PEACE.

I've never known. Was she happy? I don't mean just with me, but happy, period, happy in her life? How can you know that? Because it was always the same. Ultimately, it depends on your point of view. Sometimes she looked radiant to me. I'd tell myself that she'd finally found happiness, in spite of everything. Today I don't know anymore. It was just my impression, and that's not worth anything. Only reality counts. So why hadn't I ever bothered to ask her?

In the end, I let my head break the surface and saw that I was far from shore. I'd drifted several hundred meters away. Once again, it was tempting. I kicked out and realized I wasn't making any progress. The current was dragging me down. I had a sudden vision of my body lost offshore—and what I saw had an effect like a whiplash. Everything in me woke up. Adrenaline flooded every muscle. I made some broad, sweeping strokes, and things improved. I was advancing, and the sea was throwing me out. Then the effort became too much, too hard. I wondered if I'd be able to make it.

It was strange, and everything was turning in front of my eyes. Blurry visions of those I'd be leaving behind. There was François, and then Lucille's parents. I was surprised, because they didn't seem pleased. I saw some things I would never have imagined. On the sea floor, there was my black cab.

I went under, I couldn't even see the beach anymore. I was giving it all I had. Suddenly Pierre appeared. Someone explained to him that I had died in the sea. He didn't cry, he just shook his head. "Drowned?" he asked. "Impossible." I was the one who had taught him how to swim. "That makes no sense," he kept repeating.

I struggled harder and harder. I struck out with my arms, with my legs. Because I was bound and determined to see him again. I've never believed in a higher power, but I made my supplication all the same. It wasn't easy, what with all that water in my mouth. "Please, let me see him just one more time." I was ashamed, it was like being pounded in the stomach. Ashamed of running away, of my morbid thoughts. And I didn't want to pay too dearly for them, so I swam hard; my entire body was thrashing around in the foam. I felt myself getting wearier and wearier, and it made me feel like crying. I pushed harder, and I had the impression that I was dragging up everything I had left. One last stroke, so I would have no regrets. And then I felt a shock against my shoulder. My hand slammed into sand, and I raised my head. I was face down, flat on my stomach in eight inches of water.

7

"*Excuse me?*"

Her voice unnerved me a little. It also scared me. First I heard the surprise in it, and then the touch of indignation. I disregarded her tone. She shouldn't see the flaws. My fright, for example, and my inner doubts. If she noticed those, there was no chance.

I explained again, as clearly as possible. I wanted her to play an editor. Employed by a publishing house, and in charge of the manuscript submitted by one Pierre Marès. It wasn't so complicated. She had to meet with my son once or twice. Make him understand that things were moving along. The same thing she usually did, in other words. After all, that was her profession, wasn't it? Nothing to it. Everything the same, except make-believe.

She made a face. I said I understood the difficulty, but I didn't know anyone else. And besides, she'd be paid well. Yes, that wouldn't be a problem. I was ready to cough up whatever it took.

She adjusted her glasses. She was shaking all over. Mute anger. Understandable enough—I was backing her into a corner.

"I . . . I can't."

I calmly asked her why not. She said she couldn't condone my plan. I sensed that she wanted to say more, but she held back. I said that wasn't a problem. She said yes it was. I said no it wasn't, leaning in. It was kind of ridiculous.

A heavy silence set in. We were playing this game at her place, and I couldn't take it anymore. I was worried, but not without resources. I hadn't tried actors yet. I could always find one who was out of work and ready to take on the role.

"What you're asking . . . it doesn't make any sense. The book doesn't exist . . . and besides, I'm only an editorial assistant. How do you expect me to—"

"Do you really think that's important?"

She didn't take me up on that. I could see the fear in her eyes, so I pressed harder.

"Who gives a damn about that? You know this profession, you're in the best position to play the part. I'm not asking you to agree with me. I'm asking you to help me."

"You're asking me to lie."

I shook my head. "I'm asking you to tell him what he wants to hear."

My skull ached. I didn't like the turn things were taking. There was no need for me to justify myself, not to her. I didn't give a damn about what she might think. I felt like getting up, telling her to go fuck herself, heading for the government employment center, and hiring a temporary worker. But I didn't dare. I decided I couldn't trust actors, they'd take too many liberties with the role. And besides, if an actor was out of work, that meant he or she wasn't any good.

I murmured, "Don't worry. In any case, it won't last very long. He's in the terminal stage."

That time it was horror that I saw pass over her face. She averted her eyes and capitulated.

She made it clear that she didn't want anything. No instructions, no explanations, and especially no money. She told me she'd visit him only once, and even that was going too far. She would be alone, she said, on a day of her choosing. And I must never call her again.

I replied that one time wasn't much.

"Take it or leave it."

I agreed.

It took her four days to decide to visit Pierre. I went to see him at the hospital every morning. When I told him an editor was going to drop in, he thanked me. That struck me as odd. Thanks. For what? I nearly asked him the question.

The four days were long. Pierre wanted her telephone number; he said he didn't have very much time. He repeated that, and I felt something like a fire in my chest. In the end, I got upset. I told him he had to chill out. I said he had enough time, she was going to come, I hadn't raised a capricious son. I yelled, and that calmed him down.

All the while, I acted like a guy sure of himself. I tried to soothe him, but deep down inside, I was scared to death. I hesitated to call her. I was starting to really get worried, but she finally kept her word.

It was the fifth day. When I stepped into the room, Pierre greeted me with a smile I didn't think possible anymore. He was so beautiful, there on the bed, with joy splitting his face. It came down on me like a ton of bricks and almost made me lose my balance. The bright white of the walls turned dull. Or rather, he had become so luminous that he outshone everything else. My son. He wouldn't stop talking. He was like an insane person. "A book." He kept repeating those two words. "Can you imagine, Dad? They're going to make it into a book! I'll have my name on it. Like this, under the title: Pierre Marès. Unless I use a pseudonym... But no. Pierre Marès, that'll be perfect. And that's not all: I'm going to dedicate it to you! *For my father.* Or *To my father.* What do you think? Which do you prefer? It's up to you!"

He kept talking nonstop, and I could barely see him. I was floating, I swear I was floating, we were both floating. There was no more bed, no more cancer, no more plastic tube. He talked about his book, and I believed in it too. That book existed. At that moment, in that room, between ourselves. It wasn't his dream anymore, or my lie. It was a book. Like he'd said. With "Pierre Marès" under the title. And a dedication inside.

I don't remember the rest. I left when they came in to get him ready for the night. I was groggy, dazed with happiness. I barely heard the nurses. Someone put a hand on my shoulder, gently. I kissed Pierre. He was laughing, I've forgotten why. I went out backward, so I could enjoy the sight of him as long as possible. When I crossed the threshold, he called out, "See you tomorrow." I went down the corridor. As I got in the elevator, I was still laughing. I saw an orderly approaching, so I blocked the door with my foot. He was going to the ground floor too. I pressed the button. He gave me a sidelong look, and I could sense that he was uncomfortable. I was still laughing, I couldn't manage to stop. I told him that I was sorry, that I understood his discomfort. It wasn't polite to giggle like that in a hospital. He frowned. He asked me if everything was all right. I asked him why, and he placed a hand on my arm.

"You're crying."

8

I saw them too late. I already had one foot in the room, and they turned toward me. It would have been ridiculous to go out again, but I was tempted. They surely must have noticed the little pause in the middle of my step.

Lucille's parents were there, looking at me without saying a word. I held out one hand to the grandfather and waved in the old lady's direction with the other. Pierre was asleep, lying on his side, with one corner of the bed covers wedged under his right shoulder. The silence was heavy and thick. I think we were all waiting for someone else to decide to talk. My eyes were riveted on my son, and that made me feel as though I could remain silent. A nurse came in. We moved aside so that she could change the IV bag. As I watched her work, I told myself I could seize the opportunity to escape.

"We don't often see one another."

It was the old man who'd said that. It didn't sound like a reproach. I paused for a while before replying.

"I...I work a lot. And then, with Pierre and the hospital, there's not much time left."

I hated myself for explaining that to him. Justifying yourself is admitting you're wrong. I had nothing to prove to him.

"Yes, of course. Forgive me."

Hearing him apologize made me uneasy. Pierre wasn't waking up.

"He fell asleep shortly after we arrived," the old man informed me. "We haven't seen a doctor. Is there...is there any news?"

He raised his eyes. This time, nothing showed in them but the pain he was feeling inside.

"No, not really." I swallowed quietly and peered out the window. "It's not looking too good..."

The end of my sentence dissolved into the whiteness of the walls. I had the feeling that I owed the old couple more—they had a right to know. But I didn't have the strength. I jumped when he said, "And you? You okay?"

I said I was fine, I was bearing up. It was easier to talk about me, and so I did. I told him about my taxi, the night shifts, the price of parking at the hospital. I grumbled, and that relaxed him.

A nurse announced that visiting hours were over. I kissed Pierre on the forehead and joined the old couple, who were waiting for me outside. We walked down the corridor, three abreast. I wondered if tragedies brought people together. I thought not: it was just what people called "empathy"; it was just that being nice to the father of a sick person was viewed as proper behavior. I had an urge to be alone in my taxi, to drive around without any passengers.

"Will you come and have dinner with us?"

I had almost reached the car when he made that proposal.

"I've got to work, I—"

"Come on, let's go. Just for an hour. My treat."

It was only about a ten-minute drive. I had the feeling he was familiar with the place he was leading me to. Since Pierre's hospitalization, I'd managed not to run into them, but Pierre had told me his grandparents came to see him. That was good, I thought.

I followed them into a restaurant parking lot. It was one of those big chain restaurants, the kind you often find by the side of a highway. I got out of my cab and went to open the grandmother's door. She didn't thank me. She didn't smile, either—I don't remember ever seeing her smile.

The interior of the restaurant was all red velour. The floor, the seats, even the chair backs. Balloons attached to strings were floating more or less everywhere.

A waiter pulled two tables together and we sat down. They were both facing me. I thought it looked like an interrogation.

We dived into the menu because that was a way to avoid conversation. I ordered steak tartare and a draft beer. The old lady struggled to decipher many of the menu items.

I observed her and thought she resembled her daughter. The eyes, maybe the nose—and a bit of everything else, no doubt. The more I studied her in detail, the more it stuck in my throat. I wasn't sure I wanted that. The emotion, the memories. I asked myself what I was doing there.

Finally, when the waiter came back a second time, she ordered a salad. She laid her menu aside, and I was reassured to see her face return to its usual glumness.

We waited. I could see that I had no more excuses, so I asked about the dog.

"He's just fine."

I sighed. I wondered if he was doing it on purpose.

"He's getting pretty old, don't you think?"

"Oh yes, yes, of course, he's tired a lot. But he's hanging in there!"

He'd said that almost joyfully. I promised myself to finish off that dog next time I passed by their house. All I'd have to do is run over him and play innocent.

There was a brief silence, and then the grandfather's face brightened. "Pierre told us about his book. That's really good news!"

This landed on me like a punch. Of course Pierre had talked to them about his book—he talked to everybody about his book. I scrutinized the old man. His eyes were glistening.

It suddenly occurred to me to wonder if he knew. Had he brought up the subject to embarrass me? He put an arm around his wife's shoulders. It made a strange impression—as if they were now not two, but one. My pulse quickened. I was afraid, I took a deep breath. No, that was stupid, he couldn't possibly know.

"Yanis? Are you okay?"

I jumped. I drank a sip of my beer and tried to put on a good face. "Yes, yes, forgive me. You're right, all this news about Pierre's book is fabulous. But you know, he deserves it!"

The grandfather nodded, and it seemed to me that the old lady was smiling too. That made her look like Lucille again. But what got into me? I fixed my eyes on my glass and started talking at top speed.

I told them it hadn't been easy. In the beginning, I said, Pierre had asked me to submit his manuscript everywhere. The wait had been interminable. First there were letters of rejection. And then, one day, bang, we had a winner! How it had happened was incredible.

"A woman called me up to sing Pierre's praises. Like he's already a great writer, the book's going to be a hit, that sort of thing. I have to say, his book really is very good! I think a lot of editors will be kicking themselves..."

They were both staring at me and looking fascinated. I realized that I had an untouched plate in front of me.

"And when is it going to come out, this book?" the old man asked.

I hesitated. "I...actually, I'm not sure. Publication is a very long process, you know."

"Pierre...a writer!" he gasped admiringly. "It's a shame Lucille's not here to see this!"

There was no more animosity, no more anything. I was rattled. I told myself that maybe the situation we were in didn't allow us to replay old grudges. The more I thought about it, the more it seemed to me that I couldn't measure up. Tears came to my eyes. All on its own, the question sprang out of my mouth: "How do you do it?"

The old man looked me over for a moment. "How do we do what?"

"About Lucille."

I told them about my doubts, about the hours I'd spent torturing myself. In a shaky voice, I confessed that there had been nights when I'd fantasized about the police calling to say yes, they finally had proof, she had intended to die. I talked about the other nights too— the times when I'd wished for the opposite. I confided to them that I was fine with suffering, I could take it, but suffering normally, in a way already marked out by others. I didn't give a damn if she'd killed herself or not; what I wanted was to know, just to know, because not knowing was driving me crazy.

Silence fell again. I was already regretting my words and feeling ashamed. I was about to get up from my seat when the old man murmured, "Lucille died in a tragic automobile accident, Yanis. It was none of your doing, it wasn't your fault."

I shook my head. "No...It's not that...Pardon me, I shouldn't be talking to you about it. It's just that...it's so hard..."

I was afraid I was making them feel sorry for me. I didn't want that.

The grandfather's eyes were glistening. A sob escaped his throat when he tried to talk. His wife put a hand on his arm and leaned toward me.

"It's like a box, Yanis."

There was something in her voice. A hint of tenderness. The same tones as Lucille, I think, but I'm not sure.

"What's like a box?"

"This whole story," she replied. "This story is a box you can't open."

The old man sat up straight again. He'd recovered his calm.

"What she means, Yanis, is that the truth died with Lucille. Forever. Now there are only some suppositions. Some maybes, and the weight you decide to give them."

I tried to pull myself together. I was hot, sweating under my shirt.

"Right, I agree," I said nervously. "We'll never know. That much is true, no doubt about it. But how is it possible to live with that, damn it!"

I had practically shouted. My words were addressed to him, but it was the old lady who answered me: "You choose."

I stared at her, uncertain whether she was mocking me. Her dour appearance remained unchanged, and I found that impressive. Her eyes, however, seemed to be getting rounder.

"How do you mean?"

"You choose. Or, if you prefer, you invent the truth."

"What?"

I couldn't grasp her meaning, but I had the feeling she was talking down to me. Frustration was making me numb.

"The box is closed, Yanis. Forever."

Enough with the box! That outburst was seething inside of me, but I kept it there. I didn't want to get upset in a restaurant.

"It's closed," the old woman repeated. "You can't spend your life wondering what's inside! No one can live like that...and that's the reason why you have to choose. There's no other solution."

She had raised her voice. I'd never heard her talk like that. I tried to concentrate, but my head ached.

"You want *me* to decide what reality is? No...I can't do that..."

"Of course you can! You're already doing it for Pierre..."

She hadn't looked at me when she said that. I got up, left some bills on the table, and walked out.

9

I had almost reached my car when the old man caught up with me.

"Wait, Yanis. I'm so sorry. My wife meant no harm."

He grabbed my arm. I jerked it to shake him off, but he tightened his grip.

"Listen, I know it hasn't always been easy between us, but you can believe me about this: Lucille was our daughter, we suffered at least as much as you did. For her mother, it was atrocious. So all this stuff about the box, you see, that's her trick, that's her way of muddling through. Others may find it absurd, true enough, but I think I understand her. After all, not knowing, that may be a kind of luck. There are so few things in life you really choose... So why not decide for yourself, just once? Decide on reality, *your* reality, the one you've chosen? It won't be worth less than any other one, don't you think?"

As I didn't reply, he moved closer to me, murmuring,

"We just want to help you, Yanis. Both of us. What's going on with Pierre must be—"

"Thanks. It's nice of you, but I don't need anything." I jerked my arm abruptly. He released me, and I got into my cab.

I drove without stopping. My hands were gripping the steering wheel so tightly that I could feel the rigidity in my muscles at every curve. I thought about the old woman, about Lucille, about the box-and-reality business. I thought about Pierre.

The taste in my mouth was complex, hard to define. A terrible bitterness that wouldn't go away. I took a stick of chewing gum out of the pocket in the door and chewed with all my might.

I parked in front of the all-night bistro where I knew I'd find François. His team was playing a European Cup match, and he never missed such a contest. One day, accompanying his words with big gestures, he'd told me, "Other matches, I can listen to them on the radio, but not those! They're too important."

I stepped inside and there he was, sitting with his elbows on the bar in the best spot for viewing the screen bracketed to the wall. He was drinking a half-pint of beer. I ordered the same.

"Hello, old pal!" he exclaimed when he saw me.

"Hello."

"You're here to watch some soccer? You won't be sorry—we're already ahead, one to nothing."

I didn't say anything. He went back to concentrating on the match. I still had that knot in my stomach, and the old lady's words echoing inside me.

"François?"

"Hmm?"

"You think there's such a thing as a good lie?"

He didn't take his eyes off the screen; the ball he was following flew over the crossbar. He said, "A good lie?"

"Yeah. I mean, do you think there are situations where it's better to tell a lie?"

"Like when you're trying to score with a girl?"

"No, no."

"Hustling a customer?"

"No, not that either. A situation where you lie because it's better for everybody. So no one gets hurt, for example."

"Ah…"

Once again he sat up straight, his nose pointed at the screen. He froze for an instant, and then he sighed. "Shit…pretty close."

I felt like getting out of there. He turned to me. "Sorry, Yanis. So, useful lies, is that it?"

Useful. I didn't like the word. I had said *good.*

"You haven't told Lucille's parents about Pierre's cancer, is that it?"

"What? Of course I have! They know all about it, I swear!"

He looked reassured. I rubbed my eyes. Deep down, I was no longer sure of what I meant to say. I tried to explain, and he shrugged. "It's complicated…," he murmured. "Maybe you have to ask the question the other way around."

"The other way around?"

"Well, you see, what you're telling me, I understand what you're getting at. You want to spare other people, is that it?"

I nodded.

"Okay, when it's said like that, of course it sounds fine. But if you turn the thing around? For example, do you like being lied to?"

I muttered that it depended, that it wasn't the same thing.

"That's what you have to ask yourself," François went on. "Would you, in the same situation, prefer to hear the truth? Me, I wouldn't want people telling me fibs...no matter what the circumstances were! It's a question of respect, you see."

I murmured a "yes" as I massaged my brow. I had a headache that wouldn't stop.

"What is it, Yanis?"

"Huh? Nothing."

He was staring at me, a stern look I'd never seen on his face before. I stammered, "Nothing, nothing, I swear."

"If there's something, I'd rather you told me."

I repeated that there was nothing for him to worry about. I don't think he believed me, but he didn't insist. "Come on, old buddy," he said, turning back toward the TV. "Don't worry about things so much. Here, check out the match: we just scored a second goal!"

10

After I left François, I drove over to the train station, looking to pick up a fare. I love the city at night. There are certain streets that aren't very well lit at all. Shadows drift along the sidewalks. I'm not afraid; the interior of my cab reassures me. I feel safe, sheltered from everything outside my little world.

The sky clouded up and rain began to fall. Lights bulged and dimmed. At an intersection, I watched through the windshield as a stoplight turned into a reddish smudge. That reminded me of an August night I'd spent with Pierre—he must have been eight at the time. We'd rented a boat for a week, an old sailboat named *Mojo*. We'd go sailing along the coast, and in the evening we'd anchor in a cove and do a little diving. That was a fabulous week. There was nobody but the two of us—isolation is the main advantage of boating. Time stretches out; there's never any real rush.

On our last day, Pierre insisted on sailing at night. I wasn't wild about the idea, but he pleaded with me. I could feel his excitement growing. I yielded, because I don't know how to say no. I decreed that we should both wear our seatbelts, and he promised, sighing, that he would.

I had planned on a brief sail, three hours at most. We'd do a loop, come back, and drop anchor just off the beach. I had no fear of the coast; I knew the sea bottoms in that area by heart. All you had to do was to beware of fishermen, who often go out at night.

I warned Pierre. I told him he had to watch out for lights. He was happy to have some responsibilities. He said, "Yes, Captain Daddy," and knelt down to keep an eye on the horizon. With a sharp movement of the tiller, I launched the boat into the night.

There was no wind. We moved along lazily; the motor made the hull vibrate. A whole lot of stars dotted the sky; you can see them so much better out there than you can in town.

Pierre didn't talk—he was staring out to sea. I looked at his back, his little hood falling over his shoulders. The boom creaked as it swung. The compass mounted in the cockpit emitted a soft glow. Northwest. We could stay on that course. Sail straight ahead, without stopping, go somewhere else. It was tempting—to tell the truth, it always is, at least a little. After all, there wasn't much holding me here. I hadn't ever really thought about it. Maybe when Lucille died, I don't remember.

I asked Pierre for his opinion. He was surprised by my question. He concentrated, and in spite of the darkness,

I could see him furrow his brow. His fingers were curled against his lips. His mother would sometimes assume the same posture.

Finally, he answered no. He had his school friends, and grandpa and grandma too. He liked it fine here. All the same, he asked me if I'd keep on being a taxi driver if we moved. I laughed. He looked worried, so I promised him that yes, I'd still be a driver. In that case, he concluded, all right, we could go. I laughed again, tousling his hair.

We were far enough from the coast, so I cut the motor. The boat started to drift. It was pleasant, that sudden silence. Just the water sloshing against the hull, our voices, and the halyards striking the mast. I went below in search of a beer, and I also got some fruit juice for Pierre. When I came back up, he was gazing at me proudly. His arm was stretched out, his finger pointing to starboard. "There," he said. "A light."

A red glow was visible on the horizon. I smiled at him and handed over the juice. Then I started the motor again and deviated from our course a little to get farther away. The light was big, maybe a passing freighter. We continued to watch it for ten minutes; it didn't grow any dimmer. On the contrary, I had the impression it was getting closer. The glow it gave off mounted higher and higher. This was some really big vessel.

I veered away at a right angle. Ninety degrees, just to get it over with. Since the light looked red, we had to be on its port side. All we had to do was to let it pass us.

"Daddy, it's still getting bigger . . ."

I grumbled a bit. The light still shone red. I continued our rotation; the boat made a U-turn. Still that red. Incomprehensible.

"Daddy..."

"Be quiet, Pierre. Let me concentrate."

I shoved the throttle forward, giving more gas. I didn't understand. Some fool who hadn't equipped his boat correctly? No, it was too big...I squinted. My heart began to beat faster.

Suddenly, a cloud passed in front of the light. I slapped my forehead. "What idiots...it's the moon, Pierrot!"

"The moon?"

He peered at the light and then turned toward me, looking incredulous. My muscles relaxed. I burst out laughing.

"Daddy—are you sure?"

I signaled to him to come and sit on my lap. "Yes, I'm sure," I said. "Look how it's passing behind the clouds."

"The moon can be red?"

"I guess we have to believe it can. We'll ask about that tomorrow. For now, we're going back in."

The next day, we couldn't find anyone who could give us an explanation. Years later, when he was in high school, Pierre came home from his classes and talked to me about a phenomenon called a lunar eclipse. I didn't understand all the details. His eyes shone with excitement.

"I'm sure that's what it was!"

It touched me to see how well he remembered that moment.

11

The first time, I strolled in on a whim. Ordinarily, I never went into bookstores, but with everything that was going on, what was ordinary had no importance anymore. It was just to get my bearings. I wanted to figure out what my son's dreams might look like.

There were books everywhere. The silence was impressive—almost religious. I would observe the customers, their ways of examining the volumes: they handled them with respect. I didn't dare imitate them—I was too afraid of being found out. Me, the know-nothing interloper. But nobody ever said a word to me.

As time passed, I started hanging out among the shelves. On the central table, an oak plank resting on two trestles, there were piles of books. The French ones on one side, the foreign ones on the other. Those must have been the masterpieces, displayed like that.

Sometimes I brushed the covers with my fingers. The boss had attached little notes to some of the volumes:

MUST-READ. I thought about my kid. Surely, that was how he imagined his own book. All those pages, and his in the middle. Pierre Marès. Stuck in somewhere among the greats. That would still look pretty cool.

Before leaving, I'd always buy a book. So I could say I had. To give a little consistency to my project. I made no selection; I picked up the first book that lay under my hand. The old fellow at the cash register wasn't very talkative. He contented himself with scanning the bar code and slipping my purchase into a bag. At bottom, maybe he knew. After all, it must have been plain to see: me and my little game, the perfect imposture.

In the beginning, I thought I'd give them to Pierre. But I didn't have enough nerve. I always remained clear-headed, I never lost my grip. I never entered the store in the hopes of finding my son's book there. No, I really didn't. I never deceived myself. His book didn't exist. It was a lie, a matter of cowardice and good intentions. Hell and its paving stones. I tried not to think about it too much. It was already everywhere I went. A layer of grime on my skin, impossible to wash off. It burned me every time I went to see Pierre. When he gave me that happy look, I caught fire.

Of course, I hated myself. Even though he was sick, Pierre clung to reality. There were so many people around him. His friends, the nurses, his doctors. Each of them doing what they could to keep him from going under. And me, I was the traitor. The one who was locking him up. Keeping him elsewhere, far from the world, already lost to reality. I'd slammed the door in his face. Farewell to the real world. I was building him a universe of sugar. The way you do for old folks, right before the lights go out. Partly out of pity, mostly because there's a terror of staying whole all the way to the end. And my son, my own son, I was keeping his head underwater. I was crying out to him, telling him to look at the stars, not to struggle too much. To take advantage of the spectacle. "Stay down there, stay under, Pierre. It's pretty. Listen to your dad."

One evening, I was feeling totally emptied out. I went into the bookstore. I hadn't been able to make Pierre talk. "He's very tired," the doctor had told me, confirming what I'd seen. I walked around mechanically, surrounded by books. I couldn't see anything anymore. I didn't even know what the hell I was doing there. My head ached so much that I closed my eyes. I felt my legs failing me, and I must have leaned on a stack of books that shifted under my weight. I spotted a stool and collapsed onto it.

That was where I was when I saw him.

Pierre. He was coming into the bookstore. I could read the excitement on his face. He was browsing among the shelves, scrutinizing them. He checked one twice. He was shaking his head. I tried to warn him, I cried out. But he didn't understand me. "Forgive me," I yelled. It was too late; my cry resounded in my head. He refused to believe it. He turned his back on me, and I wasn't able to touch him. I couldn't even move my head. He started browsing again; you could feel his frustration mounting. He picked up all the books, one by one, a process that seemed to take forever. As for me, I was paralyzed. I knew he was going to turn back around. Our eyes would meet, and the prospect terrified me.

"Do you need some information?"

It was the bookseller who snapped me out of it. It took me a little while to emerge. I wondered how long I'd been sitting on that stool. He was observing me with a worried expression. I thanked him and picked up a book at random. Once I was out on the street, I left the book on a bench.

I started to run. The air did me good. I needed to clear my head, to evacuate all the tension. I passed a couple who eyed me suspiciously. I didn't give a damn about them. Besides, they were right. It was a flight. A fall. I was running too fast and my heart let me know it, crying out inside my chest.

I would have liked to go on, because I wasn't thinking anymore. It was good to stop thought, to reflect on nothing. The pressure on my lungs, my whole body in service of the machine. There wasn't the least bit of room left for the rest. I would have liked to keep running and never stop. In the end, it nearly suffocated me. I wobbled a little before I leaned against a wall. Things were coming back to me already.

I walked on. I didn't want to go home. By turning so often, I'd managed to get lost. I came upon a park whose gate was locked. I climbed up and over it. There was a wooden bench. I lay down on it and closed my eyes.

12

The rain woke me up. The night was dark. I had trouble getting to my feet. It was not so much rain as drizzle, a low-flying cloud trapped in the city. I was drenched. I had no idea of the time. I took a quick look at my wrist, but my watch was gone.

I left the park. It wasn't cold. I didn't recognize anything anymore. I rubbed my cheeks; I wasn't fully conscious yet. A cat passed through the shine of a streetlight. I've never liked cats, but maybe it was a dog. I'd only seen a shadow splitting the light. After skirting some buildings, I turned left. I could have turned right. It was a random choice.

The sounds grew progressively louder. First the music, because the bass notes carried farther. Then I heard the noise. A terrible vibration, dozens of voices coming from the same place. I followed the sound the way you go up a creek. I felt hypnotized, drawn on by the roaring tumult ahead of me.

I came out onto a square. The crowd was concentrated on the right-hand side. The epicenter was a bar. I tried to make out its name, but I couldn't see very well anymore. There were two loudspeakers on the terrace. The decibels were running high; people shouted to make themselves heard. They brought their faces close together. Several were mechanically beating time. There was an air about the gathering: the people seemed more like a group than a bunch of strangers. I wondered if they all knew one another.

I elbowed my way to the bar. I wanted to warm my insides. I ordered rum, which I'd started to drink when I was in high school. On Thursday evenings, we'd go to Marius's place. Always the same gang. The bar owner was the only one who didn't give us any shit about our age. He liked to sit with us. I think he got bored during the day.

The bartender shoved a Ti' Punch under my nose. I would have preferred pure rum, but I didn't say anything. I hadn't specified that, and in the end it made no difference. I drained the glass. The fiery liquid went down my throat—like a whiplash all the way to my stomach. Only the first drink is capable of producing such an effect. All the same, I asked for another one and held out a bill.

Toward the end of the fourth one, I felt it coming on. I went onto the terrace, glass in hand. The bass was still pounding, more intensely. The rain had stopped, and the concrete surfaces were already drying. I saw an empty chair and sat on it. The crowd looked even more compact than before. In the midst, people were dancing in little groups. I took the time to observe them all. Smiles everywhere. Frowns, too. Both appropriate. The women closed their eyes; the men, on the other hand, kept theirs fixed on their feet. In the past, I used to like to dance. Sure, I'd never been an ace. But with the help of a little alcohol, you forget your mediocrity. All you have to do is move a bit. "Don't be so stiff," Lucille would tell me. When she was in the mood, she was a hotshot dancer. I'd hold her tight against me, and the vibrations of her body would make my head spin.

I wondered how long it had been since then. I couldn't even count the years. The rum was taking control. I felt it coursing through my veins. A hundred meters, from the stomach to the brain. I tried not to stumble as I steered myself onto the dance floor. I say "dance floor," but that's just for the image. It was a circle, an imaginary zone things converged on. Once I reached the center, I tried to shake myself to the beat. It was complicated with a glass in my hand, so I finished my drink in one gulp.

I spotted a girl. A brunette, around forty, light olive skin. She moved well and kept her eyes open. I saw her at once: eyes like I'd never encountered before. Or if I had, then only on a TV screen. She was focusing them on me, letting me admire their blue nuances. The sea was imprinted on her retinas. Gray, green, metallic reflections. I had the impression that she was laughing as she observed me. I'm sure I looked good and bewildered.

She stepped aside to light a cigarette. A smoker, obviously. Such a sensuous girl, it couldn't have been otherwise. The rum shouted at me to go over and speak to her. I resisted for a second, and then everything exploded. I charged straight at her. She watched me coming as if I was doing the obvious thing.

"Hello."

Her eyes were even more impressive up close. I made a superhuman effort to keep from falling into them. She grabbed my jacket lapel with her left hand. I think I flinched. She flicked away her cigarette.

"Let's dance?"

I didn't really hear her, there was too much noise. I read her lips at a distance of a few centimeters. *Let's dance*. I let it happen. All I had to do was follow. She moved close to me. I felt her chest against my torso and closed my eyes. Slowly, I slipped an arm around her hips. Her head dropped onto my shoulder. Her breath scalded my neck. Then the bass got louder, more intense. She backed away slightly and went back into motion. She was a good dancer. I made an effort too. I didn't want the music to end.

It started raining again; it took me a while to notice. By the time I did, it was coming down hard. People ran for shelter. She stayed where she was, clinging to me, her hair plastered against her face. I pressed my forehead to hers. The rain penetrated everywhere. They didn't turn off the sound, or maybe they did, but I could still hear it. It came from far off, behind the curtain of water. She stepped back slowly, and I turned around in a circle. I had my eyes closed. The sky burst open again. Water struck the sidewalks violently. The whole world vibrated. I felt the caress of her fingers escaping. I took a few steps, spreading out my arms. I flailed the void.

Fear took hold of me. I wanted to call her, but I didn't know her name. I started running. Lost again. One street, and then another. Impossible to get back to the square. I tried calling out, but my voice died in my throat. A shadow came up behind me and grew larger. I could feel it closing in. I looked back over my shoulder at the shadow and saw it gaining on me. I had to find the bar, the girl, the music. Hide myself with them. I turned behind a building: nothing there anymore. The shadow was already on my heels.

I heard it gather momentum, and I collapsed on the pavement.

13

I can't sleep, and I've lost my appetite. That's not very important. I must be a sorry sight—I detect too much pain on other people's faces. I could puke, if allowed. I'm having a lot of trouble at the hospital. Every time I have to look at my son, it gets harder and harder. My betrayal is in his eyes. Fortunately, it's not always a question of the book. Sometimes I get a hold of myself and we talk about this and that. As if nothing's wrong.

Sometimes I feel strong. I have the impression that this could last.

Sometimes I lie to myself too.

14

This morning I went to see Pierre a little earlier than usual. He was doing better. For a few days now, he's been sleeping more comfortably and taking proper nourishment. We talked for a while, and then I read to him. He has trouble concentrating, so I don't know if he grasped everything. All the same, I tried my best, and I think we did all right.

Around eleven o'clock, he started talking about his book. He told me the story for the umpteenth time. He said how happy he was that it was being published and asked if I thought it could be a success. "Will I see it, you think?" I felt my heart cracking, exploding into particles. No words would come out of my mouth. He'd asked his question too naturally. Without emotion.

I wasn't up to it. He gave me a grim smile and said he was sorry. "Sure I'll see it," he said, shutting his eyes. Silence returned. I felt I was suffocating, so I left the room. I didn't have the strength to kiss him.

I went to the coffee machine. I had to swallow something. To my annoyance, my leg was shaking under my pants. I wanted it to stop, and so I kicked the wall. I don't know what got into me, but I kicked much too hard. My knee jammed, and pain stabbed me like an electric shock. I think I said, "What an asshole," before I grabbed my leg and sat down.

"Is everything all right?"

Pierre's oncologist was bending down and observing me with a surprised look on her face.

"Yes, yes," I stammered.

"You're trying to break the wall?" she asked. She seemed amused.

Strangely, the tension diminished. I started breathing again, and since I felt stupid, I smiled too. She placed herself in front of the machine and pressed a button. The LONG button, I think. That reminded me that I wanted coffee too.

She sat down next to me. I hadn't expected that, but it did me good. I said nothing so as not to spoil the moment.

"Pierre's better today."

Her eyes encouraged me. I replied that yes, it was true, I'd found him more talkative than usual.

"And you, are you okay?"

I had an urge to tell her no. Just once. To be honest, to stop lying. I wanted to confess it all: that I was scared, I was even terrified, I felt obsolete, helpless, overwhelmed. I wanted to say I was starting to think that this was a catastrophe, that I was a traitor, a coward. That when all was said and done, it was me, I was the one who was killing my son.

"It's good, what you're doing."

I raised my eyes. Was she reading my thoughts? Or had I been speaking? That was possible; it had been a while since I'd had control over anything at all. I was elsewhere, disconnected from my own body. I got up mechanically, activated the coffee machine, and made a mistake. I pressed LONG instead of SHORT. I said "Shit," and sat back down.

"You know," she went on, "we talk a little, Pierre and I. He's told me about his novel. He's so proud…"

My stomach contracted. No, really, I didn't want to hear that. Not coming from her. I wanted to stop her, to raise my hand and make her shut up, to tell the truth to her, at least to her, so that she could reason with me, scold me, outline the possible consequences, explain the importance of trust for a sick person, the irreversible harm I was going to cause.

Right, that was it. She would help me. I'd admit everything, and she'd know how to manage the situation. I just had to say it. Just make an effort. Have a little courage.

Someone called out to her from the end of the corridor. She wished me a good day and moved away with her coffee cup in her hand. I still had time. I could call her back. She'd turn around, it was my duty to tell her. But I did nothing. Because I'm weak. Because shame and fear had long since ruined me. I understood it in that instant. I stayed where I was, pathetic, leaning against the machine.

When I could finally move, I decided to leave. A nurse caught up with me at the end of the corridor.

"Mr. Marès?"

I turned around. It was Rosalie, the young nurse who took care of Pierre. I smiled, I think. I don't know what effect that produced.

"May I speak to you?"

She seemed nervous, looking around in all directions. It appeared that she was choosing her words, and then she shook her head.

"Pierre's book..."

I stopped breathing.

"It's not really going to be published, is it?"

I froze. Literally. Then I stammered, "What are you saying?"

She avoided my eyes. She mumbled that it was just an intuition, that it wasn't serious, but that maybe we could discuss it. She wouldn't stop apologizing. Nevertheless, she said, it seemed to her that there could be other solutions. Wouldn't I like to talk about them with the staff psychologist?

"That's crazy."

I'd said that sharply. Now she was looking at me with a sad expression that was hard to bear.

I turned around and pressed the elevator button. Several times.

"Mr. Marès...I'm...I'm sorry. It's just that...well...I thought that it might be better to tell the truth..."

I did an about-face. There it was again, that truth business. It was echoing inside my skull. But who did she think she was? I felt my heart accelerate. I had to explain to her. It wasn't so hard to understand. She looked intelligent, and I had some good arguments.

However, I only managed to babble a few ridiculous sentences. She wrinkled her forehead. I could see that she was making an effort too. It was such a shame. In the end, I asked her to leave me alone. My voice sounded too aggressive. I wasn't doing it on purpose, but she couldn't know that. And besides, my head ached too much.

The elevator wouldn't come, so I thought I'd take the stairs. I had to get out of there. I felt like I was suffocating. Just as I started to move away, she blocked me with her arm and said, "Please wait..."

Her cheeks were flushed, and she had the shaky voice of a person who never makes waves. She began to talk at top speed. She told me it was dangerous. Sometimes, she said, people think they're doing right, but actually they're making things worse. I needed to pull myself together. For his sake. For mine. She said a lot of things I didn't want to hear. Her apprehension made her voice vibrate.

She kept talking, and I suddenly felt scared. A terrible fear seized me. I imagined her standing in Pierre's room, spilling everything. It was a sure thing; she was too young, too emotional. It could only end like that.

I went half crazy. It came surging up into my chest. Something more than anger: total panic. The need to do something. To make everything stop. She has to shut up, I thought. Reason was out the window. I wanted her to shut up.

I took a step toward her, and I could clearly see the terror in her eyes. She started yelling, and that was like an alarm, awakening me to my madness. My ears started ringing; I was too hot. I heard raised voices. I think people were coming from the end of the corridor. All the same, I had enough time to see the walls closing in around me before I collapsed on the floor.

15

I woke up under the stern gaze of a nurse's aide. I was lying on a bed in what I guessed was an on-call room. I tried to sit up, but she stopped me.

"Wait a few more minutes."

She offered me a lump of sugar, which I refused. Nevertheless, she pressed it into my mouth. I didn't resist, and I let it melt on my tongue.

The doctor came in. The nurse's aide got up, and they had a brief discussion. They whispered, but I wasn't listening. I felt the cloud in my head breaking up.

After a few minutes, the nurse's aide left, and the doctor came and sat down beside me. That was the instant when it all came back. My mouth spoke the words on its own. Like a supplication.

"The nurse! You have to stop her from—she's going to see Pierre and—"

"No, no, calm down. Pierre's asleep. Nobody's going to see him. You have to get hold of yourself, Mr. Marès.

Rosalie is an intelligent girl—she simply wanted to discuss the matter with you. She would never go to see your son and tell him anything like that. We're professionals, we try to help our patients and their families."

I was ashamed. I could see the nurse's terrified eyes. What was I turning into?

I murmured, "You know, she's right about the book. It doesn't exist. It hasn't ever existed."

She didn't blink. "No one's going to say anything. Don't worry."

"You don't think he has to be told?"

I wondered why I was so insistent on hurting myself. She thought about the question, and then she said it was none of her business. There was something reassuring in her tone of voice. Not for the first time. My circulation was starting to come back.

"I already told you: I think what you're doing is a good thing."

"It's good to lie to a sick person?"

"That depends."

"On what?"

"On everything."

I sighed, because I can't stand phrases that don't mean anything. I said that masking reality was always a rotten thing to do, and she replied that there wasn't just one single reality. "It depends on your point of view." I didn't answer. I didn't see what she was getting at. She asked me if I knew about Schrödinger's cat. I said I didn't know

Schrödinger, so there wasn't much chance I knew anything about his cat. She smiled. That made me happy.

She explained to me about the cat. It was a thought experiment: you couldn't carry it out, you had to imagine it. The concept had been described by a scientist—Schrödinger—to illustrate the paradoxes of quantum physics.

"A radioactive atom is put inside a box. It's known that this atom has a fifty-fifty chance of decaying. A distinctive feature of quantum physics is the assertion that observation affects outcomes. Broadly speaking, as long as no one looks inside the box, the atom is simultaneously intact and decayed. Do you see the idea? The particle is in neither one state nor the other, but in both at the same time."

"I…I think I understand, vaguely…but I don't see what that has to do with the cat."

"I was coming to that. Now imagine that a cat is also placed in the box. If the atom decays, it kills the cat."

"The atom kills the cat?"

"Yes. For example, you can imagine that the disintegrating atom releases a poison."

I sensed that she was about to reach the conclusion, so I concentrated as hard as I could.

"So what does all this mean?" she murmured, leaning toward me. "If you grant, as we just did, that as long as the box is closed, the atom is simultaneously intact and decayed, what about the cat? That would mean that it's simultaneously alive and dead!"

This time she'd lost me. I opened my eyes wide, and she went on: "Quantum physics was developed to describe the infinitely small, which is, essentially, atoms. It says that measurement, or observation if you prefer, has an influence on what's being measured. In other words, the object, and therefore its reality, cannot be separated from the conditions of observation. And this theory is demonstrated by many real-life experiences! Do you understand?"

"I think so..."

"Schrödinger doesn't say that this conclusion is false. He's simply demonstrating a paradox by confronting the infinitely small with our world, the one we know. If quantum physics is correct, the cat in the box is half dead and half alive...Obviously, that's not possible. Or, if it is, then we have to reconsider our entire conception of reality."

I had the impression that she was speaking more to herself than to me. But I was wrong. She finally turned and looked at me.

"It's something like the case with your son, isn't it? If you consider that reality is dependent on the observer, then why would his be less real than any other?"

There was tenderness in her eyes. And warmth. I murmured, "Yes, I think I really like your box story...even though I've never liked cats."

She laughed softly. "You know, I'm certain the Schrödinger experiment would work just as well with a dog."

16

I was sitting in my taxi. I'd left Pierre two hours before.
It was more and more painful, every time. The telephone
rang, and I wasn't surprised.

It was the doctor. She simply asked me to come to the
hospital; she said I would probably have to stay the night.
There was nothing else to add. I understood immediately.
I liked her manner of speaking to me. It wasn't really professional anymore.

I turned off my roof light—I could make the drive
alone, without any passengers. That wasn't important now.

I parked in the lot and went up into the building. Inside the elevator, I leaned against the wall. I took a deep
breath, but I couldn't detect any hospital smell anymore.
That was normal, I'd grown used to it—I'd been coming
here for four months now. The doctor greeted me outside
the on-call room. She gave me a few details that I didn't
listen to. "No one will disturb you," she said. That was the
only thing I heard.

I opened the door. The room was bright, filled with the last rays of the setting sun. Pierre was lying half on his side with a plastic tube in his mouth. He looked too small. I closed the door behind me and stepped into the room. Outside, two voices were having a confrontation in the parking lot. I closed the window and the shouting stopped. I stood in front of the armchair. I'd spent so much time in that chair during the past few months; it was sucking me in. I pulled it close to the bed and sat down.

I turned my eyes on my son. I took my time; I wanted to examine him in detail. He was breathing with difficulty. There were long pauses between his breaths. He looked beautiful to me, there on his bed, an incredible dignity about him. He had a fight going on inside. I could tell by his creased forehead, by his drawn features: an indescribable rage, a great clash. One last blow for honor's sake. And my Pierre, he was a general. A war chieftain of uncommon valor. *To the death.* From where I sat, I could hear his cry.

I shivered. I realized that I was proud of him. This kid was my greatest accomplishment. What he was made my life a success. I thanked Lucille, barely moving my lips. They didn't produce the smallest sound, but it was important all the same. I took his hand. He blinked slightly, and I told myself that maybe he could hear me. Or he could feel me. That was enough. Then I started to talk.

I told him the story of his life. The whole story, all the way. I told him how he'd finished his studies and become a biologist. And then that girl, how crazy that had been. The shock in his chest when he'd met her. Beautiful as the night, she was, a kind of miracle. Their happiness when they'd moved in together. And their son too. My pride when he'd placed the baby in my arms. Me, a grandfather. Do you remember, Pierre, do you remember how moved I was? I also told him about the hard times, because life never turns out exactly the way you wanted it to. And about how they'd overcome every problem. He'd been battered, but he'd picked himself up. And in time, he'd become an extraordinary man. A good, decent, brave guy.

And then I told him about his writing career. Oh yes, of course, what a writer he'd turned into! The books he'd published, his happiness every time, and every time the same. We were all so proud of him. His wife, his children, and me. When all was said and done, life hadn't been so bad. Had it, Pierrot? And then, about when it came time for me to go. His terrible sorrow. And how I'd consoled him, how I'd told him it was normal, it was in the order of things, and it was best that way. And how I was leaving happy, because I had had such a son.

I talked without stopping. I told him everything, explained everything. I gave him back his life. Somebody had to give it back to him.

Night fell. It came upon us like that, just as we were making up for all the lost time. It settled in silently, and I think it was listening too. It let me put things back in their proper places, without saying anything, without looking at me funny. When I finished, it got up. It stretched infinitely, smiling as one does after a good story. It saluted me discreetly. And then it left with my son.

17

In the morning, I got into my car. I hadn't slept. I had the feeling that I was floating alongside my body. I drove fast. It was exhilarating. I thought that Lucille must have felt the same sensation before she missed her last curve. The idea pleased me. I saw flashes of light, but they weren't important.

I reached the edge of the water. The sky was gray, the sea covered with metal. There was no wind and barely a hint of a swell. I rented a Zodiac for the day. I could see that the boat guy was suspicious. All the same, he gave me the keys. He must have told himself it wasn't his problem.

The motor was powerful. It took me only three hours to reach the Island. I stopped in the middle of the cove. My inflatable boat was gently rocking. I dropped the anchor. The water depth was twenty meters. I lay down for a moment to clear my head. It was hard, because everything was scrambling around inside there. Too many images. Pierre. Lucille too. I breathed slowly, and I felt my rhythm, in spite of everything, slowing down. I wanted that to last awhile.

I slipped into the water, one hand on the rope that ran the length of the Zodiac. The weight under my ribs was pulling at me. I'd put twenty kilos on my diving belt. I was wearing neither a wetsuit nor flippers. I felt cold, but that quickly passed. It was as though a magnet was drawing me down. When I let go of the boat, the result was immediate. I plunged into the void, descending in a straight line to the bottom. Little by little, my descent slowed. The pressure reclaimed its rights. I decompressed, and the belt became lighter. It took me almost a minute to reach the sea floor.

I'm lying on my back. The column of water is crushing me, but my body gradually grows used to it. The descent cost me no effort, so I've still got some time. The light above me started to fade after the first few meters. There are too many particles in suspension.

The sky is white. Strange. It's been so long since I raised my head. To my right, a shadow passes. I shift my eyes and spot the anchor. It's a few meters away. The chain drags along the sea floor and then rises up to the surface. At the other end, the Zodiac is calmly drifting. Seen from down here, the boat's a big blur. The surface distorts its proportions. It looks as though a seagull has landed on the back of the boat, but I can't be sure. Maybe it's the motor, which I'm seeing from an unusual angle. In any case, I'd rather it be the motor. I'm not crazy about seagulls.

Beyond twenty meters of water and dust particles, the world seems to expand. It swells up, it hesitates. I'm not really a part of it anymore. I observe it disappearing, and it's as though I could invent it. Because I can no longer see it, I make of it what I want. I can draw parallel lines from here. I watch them heading off into the infinite, and it's beautiful enough to gouge out your eyes. I see flashes of white. There's no more seagull, no more motor. I feel fine.

ACKNOWLEDGMENTS

Thanks to Éléonore, Soazig, and Vanessa for their invaluable support.

Thanks to Alexis and Rosalie for having brought the hospital to life.

Thanks to Aïda, for all the rest.